Mahoney

and

Me

Mary Lee Tiernan

Mahoney and Me

First Paperback Edition
June 2013

ISBN-13: 978-1490446103
ISBN-10: 1490446109

Mahoney and Me is a work of fiction. The characters and events in this book are fictitious. Any similarity to real events or to real persons, past or present, is coincidental.

Author photograph by Lynne Flower

Mahoney

and

Me

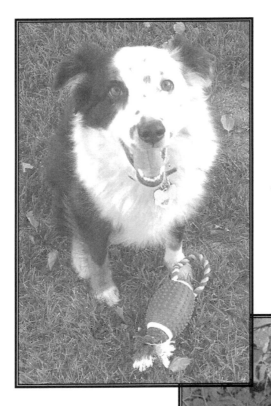

Dorsey

Charlie

Chapter 1

Mahoney stopped the car at the top of the driveway and cut the engine. Dorsey barked happily in the backseat. "I'm home, I'm home. Let me out." Mahoney slid out of his seat and opened the rear door. Dorsey exploded from the car.

I didn't move. I sat staring at the house.

Mahoney slid back into his seat. "What's wrong?"

"Your house looks different. I mean it's the same, but it's different." I shrugged. "I can't explain."

"That's because it's not *my* house."

I finally broke my gaze and turned toward him.

"It's not *my* house," he repeated. "It's *our* house." He leaned over and pecked me on the cheek. "Welcome home."

I came 'home' like a pauper with one small suitcase of personal items. All new. Everything else I had owned, including my house, my car, and my van-camper, had been blown up by a madman less than two weeks ago. I was supposed to have been in that house when it turned into a fiery inferno. I shivered.

Mahoney reached over and smoothed back my hair from my face. "Don't think about it."

"How can I not think about it?"

Instead of answering, I guess there really wasn't an answer, he got out of the car, walked around it, and opened my door. He held out his hand, which I took, and he helped me out of the car. He wrapped his arms around me and said, "I love you."

That's one of the things I like about Mahoney. He cuts to the chase. No platitudes like 'It's going to get better with time' or 'We're together, that's all that counts.' His simple "I love you" said it all.

He opened the trunk and retrieved my suitcase and his duffle which I took from him and put on the porch. Easy unpacking for us. One trip and we were done. But the kids' stuff—food and bowls and a kitty litter box and of course the cat carrier with Charlie in it—took several trips.

Dorsey waited for us at the front door. Woof, woof. "Hurry up. I've got to get inside and check it out." Dog-talk uses much fewer words than human language.

I paused in the doorway. A month ago, Mahoney had hidden me here while he—that's the police in his official capacity—hunted down the madman. Madmen, actually. In the end, there were three of them. I'd had to lock myself inside day and night. The house had begun to feel like a prison. "Can we leave the front door open for awhile?" I asked him.

"Sure." He understood.

Mahoney took our stuff to the bedroom while I put the kids' stuff away and let Charlie out of her carrier.

"She gonna be okay with the door open?"

"I don't think she'll go out, but if she does, we'll let Dorsey play the 'find Charlie' game." Cats generally don't like change, and every time I had to shuffle Charlie to a new location, she'd hide. I'd taught Dorsey to find her. Border collies need 'jobs;' it's in their breeding. So while he did his 'job,' I no longer had to worry about where Charlie might be hiding.

We made some coffee for Mahoney and tea for me,

poured a dish of water for Dorsey, and took them out on the front porch. Dorsey settled down at our feet, panting from the excitement of getting home and from his few minutes running around the yard and house. He'd been very badly beaten when the madman was wiring my house for the bomb and hadn't fully recovered yet.

Mahoney leaned back in his chair, put his feet up on the railing, and sipped his coffee. "It's good to be home. No, let me rephrase that; it's good for all of us to be home."

We sat in silence for a few minutes enjoying the view of the mountains. Two attempts on my life in the past month, however, had strained my ability to relax for long.

"Is it really over?" I asked.

"It's over."

"How can we be sure?"

"DNA from the body at your house IDed him as the twins' brother."

"How come he didn't make it out of the house?" Not that it really bothered me. I was more curious than anything else.

"The arson inspector said he was an amateur. He apparently didn't time it right."

I looked up at the mountains. "What if there's another brother?"

Mahoney reached over and took my hand. "Don't do this to yourself. Think of something else."

"Like?"

"Like shopping. Your half of the closet is empty. You could drop me off at work tomorrow and take the car."

"Work tomorrow? Already?"

"I've missed a lot of days, Princess. I have to go in."

When we first met and the sparks flew between us, I'd asked Mahoney how that could happen so quickly. He said it was natural because I was a Princess in need of being rescued and he a Prince Charming in need of a princess to save. I don't mind being his princess, not one bit.

"Speaking of work, I'd better check in with the lieutenant."

He raised that gorgeous body of his up from the chair, and I admired it until he disappeared through the doorway. He popped back out a minute later and handed me a pad and pen.

"What's that for?"

"To make a list of the things you need to buy tomorrow."

That was easy. I wrote down "everything."

When Mahoney came back, he picked up the pad. "Hope you didn't sprain your hand writing all this down. Hand me the pen."

I didn't. He knows how I feel about taking orders.

"Please?"

I handed him the pen. He wrote something down and handed the pad back to me. Below "everything," he wrote "sexy dress."

"Why do I need a sexy dress?"

"You have an important ceremony to attend." He broke out with a grin. "I got a promotion to senior detective."

I jumped up and hugged him. "That's great! Oh, that's wonderful!" I kissed him on the cheek and stepped backward. "I hope my case helped. Maybe some good came from it."

He wrapped his arms around me. "A lot of good came from that case. You're here with me, aren't you? The promotion's just a bonus."

I shopped and shopped and shopped, in places where the clothes fit me better than Walmart's and among other things did find that 'sexy dress.' At least it was sexy by my standards. I dress more for comfort than style and pay little attention to the 'latest.' A simple black dress, but the cut made it 'sexy.' I bought a fancy shawl for evening wear and a tailored jacket that dressed it down for business-type occasions. I like versatile clothes.

I visited Staples last and needed a cart for transporting all my purchases to the car. Computer and appropriate accessories, reference books such as the indispensable dictionary and thesaurus, paper, pens, etc. etc. I barely had enough energy to carry my belongings into the house before I flopped down on the couch.

Dorsey, however, had other plans for me. After his 'thank goodness you're finally home' greeting, he waited patiently while I emptied the car. He even carried a few of the smaller bags into the house for me. He interpreted my sitting down, however, as Dorsey time. I met Dorsey when he rescued me from a predator. A couple of weeks ago he almost died protecting me. I couldn't deny him. After a detour for 'lovins' for Charlie, we went out on the porch from where I threw the ball into the yard for a few rounds of catch. Not too many; I still had to be careful he didn't overexert himself.

A car pulled into the driveway. I turned to run into the house to lock all the doors and windows. I stopped and reminded myself that every car turning into the driveway did not mean a madman intended to jump out and kill me. Mahoney got out.

"Borrowed a car from the car pool," he said as he came up the porch steps. He kissed me and we walked into the house. "Did you go shop..." He surveyed the sea of boxes and bags piled around the great room and on the dining table. "Never mind, I see you did."

Mahoney poked around the computer boxes stacked on the end of the table and read the specs on the computer.

"Nice," he said, "top-of-the-line."

"I never know when my muse will speak to me, but when she does, I'd better be prepared to listen." I'm a writer; I call my inspiration 'my muse' after the nine Muses of Greek mythology. My stomach growled.

"I'm hungry too. I'm going to change into a pair of sweats and get cookin'."

Mahoney's a good cook—no, a great cook. Since cooking is my nemesis, my job is KP duty. While we ate, Mahoney glanced at the boxes stacked on the other end of the table, then around the room.

"Where do you want to set that up? I think up some place in here for now." He meant the great room.

"I hate facing a wall; I feel like I'm being punished." I looked around. "Any chance of in front of that window that looks over the side porch?" After dinner we rearranged the furniture to fit in a table he dug out of storage and placed it in front of the window.

"Want to start unpacking that stuff?"

I didn't. Most importantly, both of us needed to unwind. Secondly, I'd probably drive him crazy with my finicky preferences for arranging my desk. Instead, we curled up on the couch together to watch a movie. Our closeness sparked other interests, and we never did see the end of the movie. It was a wonderful affirmation that I was alive and the bomber was dead, instead of the other way around.

One day of shopping, three days to put it all away. The computer took up most of that time. I quickly hooked up the hardware, but getting all the components to talk to each other and installing programs took a lot longer. When I finished, I admired my new work space.

"Okay, Muse," I said, "you can come visit any time now. Maybe you can help me recreate that novel I'd been writing when the fire..." No, don't think about it. Focus elsewhere.

On the night of the ceremony, Mahoney wore his dress blues. "Hope this still fits," he said as he pulled the uniform from the closet. "I haven't had it on for a long time." It fit perfectly.

"How do you stay in shape? I never see you exercise or go the gym."

"The gym at the station. I go in early every morning, exercise, and shower before I'm on duty."

"You do? I never realized you leave early."

"I guess it's such a routine for me that I don't think of it as going in early anymore. The workout's simply become part of my normal working day."

I put on my 'sexy dress;' Mahoney hadn't seen it yet.

"Have you seen my..." He stopped when he saw me. "I like." He motioned a spiral with his finger, and I turned in a circle. He backed me up to the bed saying, "Maybe we should forget the ceremony."

I pushed him away. "No way."

The parking lot was jammed, and throngs of people stood around the lobby of the auditorium. Mahoney wasn't the only one being honored that night. The ceremony included all Cedar Falls P.D. officers being promoted and those receiving special recognition for performance of duties 'above and beyond.'

Mahoney introduced me to so many people that they became a blur. The only person I particularly noted was a good-looking blonde woman dressed like a fashion model. Her clothes made her stand out, but it was her actions that made me take notice. People who knew Mahoney came over to congratulate him. Her constant glancing in our direction indicated that she knew him, but she kept her distance. When people began filing into the auditorium and Mahoney excused himself to go sit in the honorees' section, she approached me.

"Hi," she said with a smile and introduced herself as Bethany. I responded in kind. "Are you the one Mahoney saved from the fire?"

That's not what happened, but I had no intention of going through that story again or of correcting her. Then I began to wonder how she knew about the fire.

"You're not planning to stay in Cedar Falls, are you?"

What kind of a question was that? She stood there with one hand on her hip waiting for an answer, so I replied as vaguely as possible. "Who knows?"

"I mean, you're just visiting temporarily, right?"

An announcement over the PA system asked everyone to please take our seats. Saved by the bell, so to speak. I hoped she wouldn't follow me in and sit next to me. She'd smiled, she'd introduced herself, all correct etiquette, but I heard a false note. Why had she waited until Mahoney left before coming over? And those questions. I didn't like her. Fortunately, with a "See you later," she moved away. I brushed her from my mind and never mentioned the encounter to Mahoney. I should have.

Chapter 2

Molly phoned. "This is Molly. I met you the other night at the police ceremony. I'm Bert Egger's wife."

Thank goodness she gave me that clue. I'm much better at recognizing faces than names, and 'Molly' by itself would have meant nothing to me. Bert Egger's name I knew from conversations with Mahoney; they often partnered together on a case.

"A couple of us girls are getting together for lunch tomorrow, and we were hoping you might join us."

"Thanks, Molly, I'd like that." And I would. I needed to make friends in my new hometown. The only people I knew, except Mahoney of course, were Jennie and Pete DeLane, an older couple who were friends of Mahoney's, and Kevin, the bookstore owner, and that was a business-only connection.

"Where and when?"

I wrote down the particulars and promised to see her tomorrow at 11:30.

"Hey, Dorsey, I have a date tomorrow. What do you think of that?"

He picked up on my enthusiasm and danced around me. Woof, woof. "What time are we going?"

Molly, Arlene, and Eileen looked vaguely familiar so I'd probably met them at Mahoney's ceremony, but they had the grace to reintroduce themselves. Not surprisingly, considering where I met them, they were wives of police offices. I liked them immediately. Friendly, easy to talk to. Our lively conversation jumped from one topic to another. "And then he told me I..." Molly's voice faltered as she looked behind me.

"Hi, ladies, how are you all today?"

I turned around and saw Beth? No, Bethany. While we dressed in casual clothes appropriate for lunch with the girls on a weekday, from Bethany's coiffed hair piled high on her head to her four-inch spiked heels, she looked as though she was on her way to the Oscars.

"Hope I'm not interrupting. I wanted to see how Mahoney's friend here," she patted me on the shoulder, "is feeling after her ordeal."

Bit of a mixed message there. She didn't use my name, didn't speak to me directly, but was familiar enough to pat me on the shoulder? I felt like a piece of the silverware sitting on the table that one picks up and examines while conversing with someone.

"I'm fine, thank you." I turned back to the table and took a bite of my dessert.

"I've got to run." In those heels? I don't think so. "See you later."

We remained silent until the tapping of Bethany's heels faded.

"What was that all about?"

I shrugged.

"Bit condescending, wasn't she?"

"Do you know her?" Molly asked.

"Not really. I met her at the police ceremony. Who is she?" I asked.

"A police groupie. She loves to hang around the cops."

"She's never bothered saying hello to me before."

"Me either."

"She's after Mahoney," Molly said. "He's never paid the least bit of attention to her, but that doesn't stop her from wishing."

"Well, she can't have him," I said. The girls laughed.

I spent the afternoon on the computer. Since my muse wasn't speaking to me yet—or maybe she was and I had too much else on my mind to listen—I put in a few hours recreating my past. I'd lost my address book, but my email account still listed my contacts. I sent emails to friends asking them to send me their addresses and phone numbers. I contacted companies with my change of address and phone number and checked on the progress of my insurance claims: house, car, and van. Boring stuff. So I was happy to hear a car pull into the driveway and gladly shut down the computer.

Mahoney drove a different car from the car pool. They take what's available. He had a hard time extracting those yummy long legs of his from the tight space of the compact car.

"I have to admit," he said after a kiss, "that I really miss my own car. How about we go car shopping for you this weekend?"

I brought him up-to-date on the progress of my claim. "I'm a little hesitant to incur that debt until I know the money's coming in to cover it."

He put his arm around my shoulder as we walked to the house. "No problem. I can cover for you."

After dinner, we spent some time together on the computer narrowing down the makes and models. I'm happy with a car as long as the engine starts when I turn the key and it gets me where I need to go. Mahoney's fussier. We narrowed the list down to a half dozen that he felt deserving of a test drive.

We rejected the first two as soon as Mahoney tried unfolding all six feet plus inches of himself into them. Tried...he couldn't do it. Number three we liked, but only ho-hum. Number four I really liked. The silver color reminded me of the color of the van I'd lost. We took a test drive, and Mahoney stamped it with his approval.

"Want to go try the others first?" he asked.

"Not really. I'm sold on this one."

Then followed the interminable paperwork and haggling over price. Mahoney handled the haggling. Finally, I drove my new car off the lot with Mahoney following behind. We went to dinner at his favorite Italian restaurant, Mipiace, where he'd taken me for our first date.

"You look sexy in that car," Mahoney said.

"Yeah, right."

He leered at me. "I like sexy."

"Princes don't leer," I reminded him.

"Don't I deserve a reward for getting you a good price on the car?"

"You certainly do, but that's dessert. Dinner first. Now put your leer away till after the manicotti."

I did keep my word and gave him his reward after we got home.

The routines of daily living, the replacement of some of my belongings, having Charlie and Dorsey to care for, lunches with the girls, and having a new home put my life back into working order. Of course, the very best part about my new home was having Mahoney in it. As my life filled back up, the demons who liked to remind me about the fire and my escape from death slowly faded into the background. I even began to recreate the beginning chapters of the novel I'd lost.

At our next girls' get-together for lunch, after we placed our orders, Eileen set a small package on the table.

"I'm sorry," she said. "This should have been delivered to you days ago, but it seems there's a mix-up with the address and the post office returned it to us." She handed the package to me.

The package had my name on it, but the address had been crossed out and someone had written: "Incorrect address - return to sender."

"The street number's wrong," I said, "but I don't understand. Why did you send me a package?"

"It's a bracelet someone bought at the shop and asked to have sent to you."

"Who bought me a bracelet?"

"That I don't know. One of the clerks put the bracelet and a note with the address where it should be sent into an envelope and left it in my workbasket. We each do our own giftwrapping and then give the package to the clerk to send to the post office. There was nothing to indicate who actually bought it."

"Who wrote down the address—the clerk or the customer?" I asked.

"I didn't recognize the handwriting, so I assumed the customer wrote it."

"Do you still have the note?" I asked.

"No. I threw it away after I finished addressing the package. I don't know if I made the mistake with the street number or the customer did, although I'm usually very careful and double-check the address."

"You didn't realize the address was wrong?" Molly asked.

"No. I've only been to Mahoney's a couple of times and that was with Bill driving. I never paid attention to the actual address, so I wouldn't have recognized the error. I was glad when I saw who the returned package was for so I could hand-deliver it. Please, open it," Eileen said.

I tore off the brown mailing paper and found bright green and yellow gift wrapping paper folded around a box. Inside the box lay one of Eileen's charming handmade creations, two strands of light green and copper beads twisted together. I took the bracelet out of the box and held it up for everyone to see.

"It's very pretty," I said.

"Didn't you think it was odd that someone bought a gift and didn't include a card or something?" Arlene asked.

"I did, so I asked the clerk. We have some gift cards available at the checkout counter. She was a bit fuzzy about the details, but said the person wanted it to be a surprise, like from a secret admirer."

"How did the person pay for it?" Arlene asked.

"I asked that too. The clerk said she paid with cash. She remembered that because the woman had a large bill and the clerk had to go back to the safe to get change."

"Did you ask her to describe the woman who bought it?" Molly asked. We girls were turning into a regular sleuth club.

"No." Eileen turned to me. "I'm sorry. But I will ask the clerk later."

"Here," I said, holding the bracelet out to her.

"Oh, no, it's already paid for and it was meant for you. It's yours. Please, keep it."

"What really bothers me aside from the unknown identity of this benefactor is how she knew where I lived," I said. "Very few people in Cedar Falls know me, much less where I live."

"Maybe it's from a fan," Arlene suggested. "Lots of people here know you as a writer."

"Possible, but not where I live."

With little else to say on the subject, our conversation drifted to other topics. I was uneasy, though, through the rest of the meal. As we said our goodbyes, I reminded Eileen to please check with the clerk and call me to tell me what the clerk said. She promised to do so.

After dinner that night, I showed Mahoney the bracelet and explained its mysterious purchase. He didn't like my getting gifts from unknown senders either.

"Did Eileen call with a description of this person?"

"Yes. Well, yes, she called. Apparently the shop was busy when the woman purchased the bracelet, so the clerk didn't pay a lot of attention and couldn't remember anything about her, not even the color of her hair."

"Have you given our address to anyone local?"

"Hmmm. I did contact some companies to update my customer info, especially the credit card companies when I asked them to send a duplicate card. But none locally... Wait! The car dealership. When I filled out those papers. But you'd think if they wanted to send me a thank you gift, they'd want me to know who sent it."

I draped the bracelet around my wrist. It was pretty.

"Do me a favor, Princess, okay?" I love when he asks. "Put the bracelet away for now and don't wear it."

"Okay, but why?"

"I don't want the sender to see you wearing it. Let her wonder if you got it or not, or whether she had the correct address."

Chapter 3

The next day all hell broke loose in Cedar Falls. Four masked gunmen in making their escape from a bank robbery shot a police officer and took a teen-aged girl hostage. The police cordoned off the city, but didn't apprehend them. Either the robbers made their escape before the police set up roadblocks, or they were still in the city. So we had four dangerous criminals possibly hiding somewhere in the city, a young girl missing, and a wounded officer fighting for his life. While the police searched, parents pleaded on the news for the girl's safe return, and well-wishers left flowers and candles outside the hospital.

Mahoney called to warn me to be vigilant and to tell me he probably wouldn't be home any time soon. Since our house is somewhat isolated, I locked the doors and windows while I was inside—an all too familiar procedure—and didn't stray far from the front door when I let Dorsey out or sat on the porch. I was grateful for Dorsey. He was my personal warning system and would let me know if someone were lurking about.

The police found the girl early the next day. The robbers had dropped her at a large park near the outskirts of town where she'd hidden for fear they would come back. She emerged from the woods when she saw the police cruisers and heard her name being called. She was frightened, cold, and hungry, but had not been hurt. The news played the footage of her joyous reunion with her parents over and over. That was the good news. The police still had not located the gunmen; that was the bad news.

As I was watching the breaking news of the girl's reunion with her family, Mahoney came home. He'd been gone over 24 hours. He held me close and kissed my forehead without saying a word. I hooked my arm around his waist, he put his arm over my shoulder, and we walked to the bedroom. I helped him undress, and he fell into bed. I pulled the sheet over him, kissed him on the cheek, and told him I loved him. I'm not sure he was awake long enough to hear me.

To keep Dorsey quiet while Mahoney slept, I took the collie for a long walk around the neighborhood. It was an opportunity for me to explore and to let Dorsey rid himself of some of his energy. Several houses down from ours, I heard a car approaching from behind us and herded Dorsey onto the lawn well out of harm's way. I didn't pay attention to the car until it slowed down. Oh, oh, I hoped it wasn't the owner of the house slowing down to yell at us for being on his lawn. I turned around.

The man driving the black car masked his features with his sunglasses and a baseball cap pulled down low over his face. He was obviously taking a good look at me.

Dorsey growled and moved protectively in front of me. The driver zoomed off. "Good boy," I told him. "You're my ace bodyguard." Woof, woof. "Thanks, Mom. I try."

By day three, the intense search for the robbers ended. The police simply did not have the staff and man-hours to maintain that kind of search. Mahoney and I were enjoying our habitual after-dinner coffee/tea on the porch. "Well, well, look who's joining us."

I turned around and saw Charlie saunter onto the porch as though she'd been doing it all her life. Yeah! A good sign she's adjusting. Dorsey went to her. Woof, woof. "Should I herd her back inside, Mom?"

"It's okay, Dorsey, she can come out. You keep track of her for me, okay?"

Charlie walked over to the steps where the railing did not impede her view and lay down. Dorsey followed and lay down beside her.

Mahoney sat in his chair, as he customarily did, leaning back with his feet up on the railing. I listened while he reviewed the major points of the case. He does that because it helps him when he 'thinks out loud.'

"We're clueless," Mahoney concluded.

"And they never said a word the whole time they were in the bank?"

"Not one. They passed notes or pointed. They didn't speak to anyone in the bank or to each other. We figured they didn't want anyone to recognize their voices, so we've been working on the angle that they might be local. Still nothing. Of course the FBI is really in charge of the bank robbery investigation, but we're working with them on it, and we still have the kidnapping and shooting." The FBI is always in charge of bank robberies since the money is federally insured.

"Why did they shoot Blakely?"

"We're not sure about that either. One of the witnesses said Blakely took a step forward, and the robber shot him. No warning or anything."

"Would robbers usually say something?"

"It wouldn't be unusual to say something like 'Stay where you are' or 'Don't take another step,' but this guy just shot. Why? Where are you going with this?"

"One more question. What did they say to the girl?"

"Didn't say anything to her either. She told us that one guy held her with a hand over her mouth, and when they reached the park, he nodded to the driver who slowed down. The guy holding her opened the door and pushed her out, and they took off before he'd even closed the door."

All of a sudden, Mahoney straightened up. He got it. "You do have a knack for tying bits of information into a new light, don't you?"

He pulled his cell out of his pocket, pushed a speed dial number, and put the phone to his ear. "Lieutenant, Mahoney here. I have an idea." He turned to wink at me for saying "I" and not "we." It's all that we can't talk to a civilian about a case business. We'd passed that point long ago when we worked together on my case. "Maybe we do have a clue. What if these guys didn't talk because they're dumb?"

Mahoney listened. "No, I don't mean 'dumb' as in 'stupid,' but 'dumb' as in can't talk—mute." He went over all the same info we just had. "Right. And they shot Blakely because they couldn't warn him verbally. They shot him because it was the only way to stop him." Mahoney gave me a thumbs up and blew me a kiss. "Yes, Sir, I'll be following this up first thing in the morning."

After Mahoney hung up, he held out his hand to help me out of my chair. "I know it's a little early," he said, "but I'm still tired from that long night I put in. However, I do have a little energy left, and on behalf of the police department, I would like to express my gratitude for your assistance on this case." Oh, goodie, goodie, I knew what that meant.

As I parked my car the next day for our girls' regular lunch date, Bethany walked up.

"Are you living with Jack?" No pretense of politeness with a 'hi' or a 'how are you' first. Just straight to the point.

And Jack, not Mahoney. Interesting.

I finished putting money in the meter and looked directly at her. "It is none of your business whom I live with."

"If it concerns Jack, it's my business." Wow!

"Perhaps your time might be better spent pursuing someone who has an interest in you." Mean, I know, but truthful.

Her face reddened. "Who says he doesn't have an interest in me?"

"He does." Not quite true, but if actions speak louder than words...

"So you've been talking about me."

"No. A third party said that."

She took a step closer to me. I held my ground.

"You don't know what you're talking about."

She looked past me then flounced away, but flung a parting remark over her shoulder. "I don't know what he sees in you."

I'm sure she didn't.

Molly stood at my side. "What was that all about?"

I shrugged. "Apparently Mahoney is interested in her, and I'm getting in the way."

"I don't like her continuing interest in you."

"Neither do I. Come on, let's go in to lunch."

During lunch, our conversation naturally gravitated toward the young police officer, his wife, and their two children aged two and four.

"He's still in intensive care," said Molly. "I don't even want to think about the medical bills and recuperation time. That poor family needs financial help."

"We need to organize some fundraisers; I'm sure the other wives would help," Eileen said. "But the typical ones like bake sales aren't going to put a dent in those bills. We need something big and different to attract interest."

"You mean like a big name to put on a benefit?" asked Arlene.

"That's it."

"Something like that."

"Well, we're got a big name sitting right here with us, don't we?"

Six eyes turned to stare at me. "Me? I'm not a 'big' name."

"Sure you are. You remember when they ran that phony announcement in the paper about your giving a talk for the police and their families? You wouldn't believe how disappointed people were when they found out it wasn't true."

"I was. I've read all your books so I was really excited about seeing you in person."

"Me too."

"And people in town were upset 'cause they weren't invited."

"It's perfect!"

"You'll help, won't you?"

"Of course I'll help," I said, "but do you really think we'd get a good turnout?"

"I'm sure the police would come out in force...oh, no pun intended."

"The public will too!"

"That's settled," Arlene said. "Let's start a list of what we'll need to do."

A date. My calendar was open, but we'd need time to plan and organize the event and schedule it somewhere. That brought up the somewhere. They bantered unfamiliar names about...this place was too small, that one too expensive. They settled on the high school auditorium. Cost of the tickets? We agreed that a lower price would draw more people. And help. We'd need lots of that.

We finished lunch with job assignments. Arlene would go to the high school to set the date and book the auditorium. Molly and Eileen would drum up volunteers. Mine was to figure out what I'd talk about. We agreed to meet in two days to start making lists of more specific needs and duties. I offered to host a meeting at my house so we'd have the space and quiet we needed. Before I realized it, the others had agreed on our usual meeting time of 11:30. Oh, oh, that meant lunch. No matter. I'd ask Mahoney where I could go to have something catered.

While we ate dinner that night, I explained our idea about my appearance as a guest speaker to Mahoney. He stopped his fork halfway to his mouth and stared at me.

Not at all what I expected. "You don't like it?"

He put his fork back down on the table and reached out for my hand. "Princess, you continually amaze me. I think it's a wonderful idea. And, of course, I, or any of the guys, will help in any way we can. Just say the word and it's done."

"You can help me with one little thing." I explained my predicament about preparing lunch for our meeting. "I'm not going to work myself into a frazzle worrying about it. Where's the best place to order catering?"

"In my kitchen? Someone else's food in my kitchen?" He almost sounded angry. Over a lunch? Then he laughed. "Just giving you a bad time. I'll fix something for you to serve."

"Mahoney, you are about to have your privileges revoked."

"I'll make it a really good lunch."

Chapter 4

Arlene was the last to arrive for the meeting. "I'm sorry if I'm late. I got held up at the vet's and haven't had time to take the boys home." The boys were her two yorkies, Elvis and Zorro. "It won't take me long. I'll drop them off and come right back."

"We're dog friendly here," I said. "Just bring them in."

"What about Dorsey?"

"He'll love the company."

"You're sure?"

"Yup."

Dorsey followed us out to her car. When he saw canine companions, he barked and jumped up to see in the window. Arlene looked skeptical.

"He's just excited to see them. Dorsey, sit." He did, but that didn't prevent him from inching his way forward as Arlene opened the door.

"Just put them down for a minute so they can all sniff hello."

Arlene did, but kept a tight hand on their leashes. I don't blame her. Dorsey must have looked like Goliath to the yorkies.

"Be gentle, Dorsey," I said.

While the dogs acquainted themselves with one another, Arlene said, "I ran into a friend of yours at the vet's."

"A friend of mine?"

She smiled mischievously. "Bethany. She had all kinds of questions about you."

"Like what?"

"Like about you and Mahoney and how long you're staying in town. I told her to ask you herself. She said she'd tried being friendly with you, but that you were too impolite."

My mouth dropped opened.

"I know, I know. I'm just sayin'."

Elvis and Zorro decided they liked Dorsey, so Arlene picked them up to carry them to the house. Dorsey danced around them and woofed. "Friends, Mom. Friends to play with."

As soon as we got inside, Dorsey raced off and came back carrying his ball. When Arlene set the boys down, Dorsey dropped his ball and pushed it with his nose toward them. Want to play? We left the host to entertain his friends while I served lunch. We worked as we ate.

Arlene had reserved the auditorium for a Friday night a month from now. That gave us plenty of time. Eileen and Molly produced long lists of volunteers.

"Everyone said yes," Molly noted.

"And now that word's getting around, I'm getting people calling me," Eileen added. "You know who called? Bethany. She was pretty adamant about wanting to join us."

They all looked at me.

"We can't very well say 'no' to anyone," I said.

"Are you sure?" Molly asked.

"Let's put her name to the side, and we'll handpick what we want her to do. Oh, and Mahoney said we could count on the guys at the station if we need them."

We made a list of all the jobs we could think of and had

more than enough volunteers to fill them so we decided to add a bake sale and a 50-50 drawing. Since I didn't know any of the volunteers, I left it to them to divvy up the names under the various jobs while I served dessert and coffee and tea.

"And now the publicity," Molly said. "My son is studying graphic design, and he's offered to do posters, flyers, or whatever we need."

"That's great. We want this to look professional."

"But he does need a photo and what the topic is."

Ah, my turn. I told Molly I'd send a photo via email and jotted down her son's email address. As for the topic, I gave them several to choose from, and we discussed each according to its general appeal.

They liked my original 'bad boys' topic, the one I'd offered for the phony appearance, but we nixed that because of the bank robbery and its aftermath. We settled on 'Characters: real or imaginary?'

"We also need articles for the newspaper. Since you're the writer, do you want to write them yourself?" Molly asked me.

I'd rather not. When I have to write about myself in the third person, it makes me feel like I'm not real.

"Why not get the reporter who did the phony article to write them? He did a good job."

"Do you think he would?"

"I'll get Mahoney to ask him. He will for Mahoney."

"That leaves us with one last item for today," said Eileen. "What do we do with Bethany?"

"Maybe she could walk around selling 50-50 tickets."

"Uh, I'd rather she didn't roam around too much." I couldn't explain why; I wasn't sure myself. "How about a ticket-taker at the door?"

"She should like that," Molly said. "Right where everyone can see her."

As the girls took their leave, they all complimented me on the delicious chicken salad.

"It has something in it that gives it a different taste, but I can't tell what," said Eileen. "Want to share your recipe?"

I laughed. "I'm strictly KP in this house, but I'll pass your compliments on to Mahoney."

Chapter 5

As I cleaned up the dishes from lunch and loaded them into the dishwasher, I gathered ideas about what I could say during my talk. My muse started talking to me. I dropped what I was doing and ran to the computer. I made notes. I opened books, found what I wanted, marked the pages, and laid the books on the desk. I added the citations to my computer notes. I did a couple of computer searches, printed off the results, and made a pile of those. I ran out of room on my desk and moved the books to the floor. In a very short time, I'd created a sea of paper on my desk and around it on the floor. When I work like that, I lose all sense of time.

I heard Mahoney's car pull into the driveway. Oh, he must be home early. I stared at my mess. Mahoney's very neat, as I am except when I'm working. I tidy up before he gets home. Where could I stash all this stuff before he...

The door opened and Mahoney stepped in.

"Hi, hon, sorry I'm late." Late?

He stopped short and stared at me and the chaos. Then he started laughing that wonderful deep laugh of his.

"You look like I caught you going through the closet to find hidden Christmas presents."

"I'm sorry about the mess...I lost track of time."

He walked over to me and peered at the computer screen. "What are you working on?"

"My speech for Blakely's benefit."

"In that case, make all the mess you want." He bent over and gave me his 'I'm home' kiss. "This reminds me I wanted to discuss something with you. Can you break away for a minute?"

"Sure."

He took my hand and led me to the rear of the house past the guest bedroom and opened an outside door. Before us, two-by-fours marked off a good-sized room. The lumber to finish the room had been piled at the top of the driveway since I'd known Mahoney.

"I was building this as a gym/office/catch-all room. But I've been thinking lately that it would make a good office for you instead."

"An office for me?" Heart, be still. I gave him my best hug.

"I might ask that you reserve a corner for a desk for me."

I grinned. "I'll see if I can spare the space." I got a swat on the butt for that.

We walked around the room hand in hand.

"I think I'll put my desk here, right in front of this window, or what will be a window."

Further on we stopped in front of a large opening, obviously for doors.

"I was going to put sliders in here with a patio outside."

"Do the doors have to be sliders?"

"No. What do you have in mind?"

"I'd love French doors."

"You mean those ones with all the little panes of glass."

"I don't think that style would go with your house. But they have French doors with just one big pane of glass."

"That would work."

I shivered from the chilly night air.

"Let's go back inside." We walked back in and closed the door. "You can come out when it's warmer. I want you to make sure you like the layout. Since it's only studs right now, we can easily make any changes you want, like if you want to move a window."

"Or put in a closet?"

"That too."

I pecked him on the cheek. "Thank you, thank you."

"Hmmm. The Prince does expect a little more in the way of thanks than a peck on the cheek."

"How about I ravage your body tonight?"

"That will do. Yes, that will do rather nicely."

We'd reached the kitchen. I'd cleaned up most of the lunch mess before my muse spoke to me, but not all of it. Mahoney likes his kitchen spotless. I jumped in front of him.

"You don't see this. Go change."

He opened his mouth to say something, closed it, and went to the bedroom to change. I quickly finished cleaning, so it was up to Mahoney standards when he returned.

He looked around. "Much better," he said and started pulling out food and pans to prepare our evening meal. I sat down at the island to keep him company.

"I know you've been really busy with the Blakely shooting, but did you ever have a chance to check with the car dealership about them giving out my address?"

"I did. Bert and I went over there and talked with the owner of the company. He assured us that all information is treated as confidential and that any employee put his job on the line if he shared the information with anyone outside the dealership."

"Did you believe him?"

"I did."

"Did you ask if he'd sent me a present?"

"I didn't ask that directly. I asked it as a general question. He said that sometimes they'll throw in a perk like a car accessory or run promos, like dinner for two at a local restaurant, but nothing personal."

"So that's a dead-end?"

"I think so."

"So where did this woman get my address?"

"I wish I knew, and I wish I knew who she was."

"Me too."

Chapter 6

While I was reading the police blotter in the newspaper the next morning, one report stood out.

"Hey, Mahoney, look at this."

"What is it?" he called from the bedroom where he was getting ready for work.

"Someone tried to break into a house just down our street."

He came out buttoning his shirt. I pointed to the report.

"Police responded to a burglar alarm at 345 Summit Drive. They found footprints in the garden below a window and a screen jimmied off. The owners were not home at the time."

After reading it, Mahoney said, "That's about four or five houses down from here."

"A little close for comfort."

At our next lunch, Molly brought a copy of the poster that her son Derek had designed. We inspected it as a group, then passed it around so we could study it up close.

"It's fabulous," I said. The others agreed.

Molly beamed. "He'll be so pleased. So is it okay if I go ahead and give this to the publicity committee to have duplicated and passed out to businesses?"

She received three 'definitely' votes.

"And I brought..." Eileen's voice faded as she leaned

down to her purse. "I brought you a little present."

She handed me a small package.

I opened the package and found another one of Eileen's creations, just as charming as the first one I'd received. For this bracelet, she'd woven strands of dark and light gray beads into a geometric pattern. I draped the bracelet over my arm.

"It's lovely, Eileen. Thank you. But let me pay you for it." I reached for my purse, and Eileen slapped my hand away.

"You will do no such thing. I understand why Mahoney asked you not to wear the first one, but I felt bad that you couldn't. So now you have one that you can wear."

"But I'd still like to pay you for it."

"No, no, no."

"Please? This is awkward."

"Tell you what. I won't take money for it, but I'd be honored if you'd wear it the night of your talk."

"And I'll be honored to wear it. Matter of fact, I'd like to put it on now. Would you help me with the clasp?"

Eileen fastened the bracelet on my wrist, and we moved on to other updates on plans for our event. Talk of the event consumed the entire lunch conversation.

After lunch, Molly and I walked together down the street toward our cars.

"So what did Mahoney tell you about Bethany working at the car dealership?" she asked.

"Say what?"

"You knew Mahoney and Bert went over there."

"Yah."

"Bert said Bethany was falling all over Mahoney. As soon as she found out we were there, she was trying to be Miss Helpful. Bert said it was really rather pathetic. Mahoney was polite but seemed a bit annoyed. I'm surprised, though, that he didn't mention her after those run-ins you've had with her."

Oh, my gosh, I'd never mentioned those to Mahoney. Why bother him with such petty stuff? And it turns out she could be the connection to someone knowing my address!

"Are you okay?" Molly asked. She stopped walking. "You've lost the color in your face."

"I never told him," I said. "I never mentioned Bethany to him. She's just weird and…"

"Jealous?"

"Maybe. I don't know. I just didn't see any point in telling him."

"You need to tell him."

We resumed walking. When we turned down the side street where we'd parked, I noticed white on my car windows.

"Molly, look at my car. Is that writing on the windows?"

We hurried to it. Jerky letters spelled out "Leave bitch."

Molly wiped a bit of the white from the window, rubbed it between her fingers, and smelled it. "Soap."

We scanned up and down the street. Cars and pedestrians passed on the main street, but the side street was quiet. We turned our attention back to the windows.

"The handwriting looks like a kid wrote it," I said.

A car drove by.

"Or an adult in a hurry before someone spotted what she was doing." Interesting that Molly had automatically used the feminine pronoun. I think we both knew who "she" was.

"I'm not driving through town with this on my windows."

"Have a rag or any tissues in the car?"

I did. Molly and I smeared the soap so the lettering was no longer readable.

"Guess I'll be washing windows when I get home."

"And telling Mahoney about Bethany?"

"I certainly will now. Thanks, Molly."

Chapter 7

The Friday for our benefit for Officer Blakely arrived. When we girls had scheduled the event a month in advance, we thought that gave us plenty of time. It had in a sense, but we were awfully busy, especially that last week. Distributing tickets and collecting money, issuing press releases, checking with volunteers to remind them about their jobs at the event, asking bakers to have their goodies for the bake sale at the auditorium by 3:00, calling the school to arrange for tables in the lobby for the bake sale and a podium on stage for me, borrowing baskets with handles and breaking up the roll of tickets for the 50-50 drawing...the list went on and on.

The only jarring note came a week before the event while Arlene and I shopped at Walmart for nametags for the volunteers and labels for the bake sale items so we could put prices on them. While we waited to checkout, Bethany strolled by.

"Oh, hi," she said. She glanced at the shopping cart. "Getting ready for the big event?" Without pausing for an answer, she asked me, "Will you be leaving Cedar Falls after your speech?"

"What kind of a question is that?" Arlene countered. Thanks, Arlene. It sounded better coming from you.

Bethany stepped back. "I was only asking. What's wrong

with that?" She tossed her head and moved away.

"Sounds like she's anxious to get rid of you," Arlene said.

Molly, Eileen, and Arlene worked all day that Friday. Except for a sound and light check with the techs mid-afternoon which only took twenty minutes or so, the girls wouldn't hear of me staying to help. The real success of the benefit, they said, depended on me, and they wanted me to be rested and relaxed. Relaxed? When they'd put that weight on my shoulders? So I spent most of the day reviewing my notes and practicing my speech.

Mahoney and I drove separately to the event. I had to be there early, and he had a few things he needed to do. I drove to the front of the parking lot closest to the auditorium doors. I was surprised at the number of parked cars I passed. The lot was filling up quickly. We had reserved a spot for me marked off by orange cones. I knew exactly where it was since I'd been there earlier for that sound and light check. But it wasn't there! Of course the parking space was there, but it was filled by another car. Not an orange cone in sight!

I had to circle around and park several rows back. Not a big thing, but annoying. Molly and Arlene met me at the door. "We were getting a little anxious," Molly said.

"The crowd's beginning to notice you're here," Arlene said. "Before they come over to talk with you, let's get you backstage. We were hoping you'd arrive before they did."

On the way backstage, I explained about my non-existent parking space and how a couple waylaid me to chat on my way through the parking lot. "But the cones were there!" Molly said. "I checked them myself about twenty minutes ago."

"Well, someone moved them."

"Do you have your notes?"

"Right here." I pulled them out of my purse.

"Do you want us to set them on the podium?"

"Let's put them on the stage manager's table, so I can give them a quick once over before I go on stage. I'll carry them on with me." We placed them on a corner of the table and left for the dressing room so the light technician could check my makeup to be sure it wouldn't shine under the lights. I don't wear much makeup, and I had added some powder as he'd requested so I didn't think it would be a problem, but what the heck.

Eileen met us in the dressing room. "Oh, you remembered to wear it. Thank you!" She meant the bracelet she'd given me. "I just took a peek though the curtain. The auditorium is filling up fast."

"Just saw the mayor and the chief of police come in," a stagehand added.

"Are you all trying to make me nervous?"

The girls stopped and stared at me. "You're nervous? Don't you do this all the time?"

"Hardly. I've been a guest speaker on occasion, but only with small groups. I've never spoken before a crowd this large."

"Oh."

"I'd like to go back to the stage manager's table and sit quietly by myself and look over my notes."

"Sure. We'll go with you and stand guard so nobody bothers you."

Molly and I led the way. Before we got to the table, I caught a glimpse of Bethany. "What's Bethany doing back here?" I whispered. "I thought she was a ticket-taker."

"I'll go find out," Molly said. She left, but Arlene and Eileen stayed with me.

We reached the stage manager's table, and I slid into a chair. I popped right back out again when I saw an empty spot on the table instead of my notes. "Where are my notes? What's happened to my notes?"

We searched the area to see if they'd fallen off the table. Nope. We asked the helpers backstage if they'd moved them. Nope. The stage manager called, "Five minutes to curtain."

I dropped into the chair, placed my elbows on my knees, and leaned down to rest my forehead in the palms of my hands. No one said a thing.

"You're on," the stage manager announced.

I stood up, gave the girls my best smile, and walked on stage. One of my professors in college once accused me of over-studying. "You know the material," he said. "Relax." Okay, Prof, a test. I had been through my notes many, many times. Now it was time to relax. I started talking and my memory opened. In a couple of places, I skipped over material I'd meant to include; in other places, I added something new that came to mind, but the speech flowed. I had to skip the quotes I planned to use because I didn't know them verbatim, so after giving credit to their authors— that part I remembered—I summarized their essence. The audience was very quiet. Listening or asleep? I couldn't tell. I noticed the stage manager flash the five minute warning. My time was almost up. I'd made it! Now for the ending.

Wanting to finish on a high note, I'd planned an unusual ending to my talk, but with everything that had gone wrong, I glanced over to the wings to make sure my special guest was ready before introducing him. He's a natural as an actor, but I had spent a little time rehearsing him for this moment. He sat patiently waiting for his cue.

"As you know, the topic for tonight is 'Characters: real or imaginary?' If you've read my book *Stopping in Lonely Places*, you know I have a special relationship with one of my characters who happens to be one of those 'real' characters. I'd like you to meet him." I looked over to the wings. "Dorsey, come here, boy."

Mahoney let go of his leash, and Dorsey bounded out onto the stage and ran to me. Woof, woof. "Hi, Mom." The audience clapped politely. I bent over to rub his head and to grab his leash. Pointing to the audience, I said, "Say hi to everyone, Dorsey."

The dog turned to face them, sat down, raised his paw, and waved it. The audience laughed.

"When I first met Dorsey, he was a stray, hungry and in desperate need of a bath, weren't you, boy?" Dorsey sunk to the floor, covered his eyes with his paw, and whined as if remembering those days. A collective "ah" rose from the audience.

I squatted down next to him. "And I was so lucky when you decided to adopt me, wasn't I?" Dorsey jumped up, put a paw on each one of my shoulders, and rested the side of his face against mine in his best imitation of a hug. Me, too, Mom, me too. The audience roared.

"Before we go, Dorsey, tell them how much they're going to like our new book."

Dorsey went to the podium, stood up on his hind legs, rested his front paws on the podium, and barked several times. It was a long speech for Dorsey. I'm not sure exactly what he said, but the audience seemed to because they laughed at all his jokes. When he finished, I waved goodbye to the audience, and Dorsey and I walked off stage. The applause was deafening. Kids and animals steal the show every time.

I'd wanted to bring Mahoney out too and introduce him, but he said if I did, he'd chain me to the bed and I'd be his sex slave for the rest of my life. With Mahoney, the sex slave part wasn't really a punishment, but I do value my freedom so I left him in the wings where he waited with open arms to greet me as I exited the stage. After my hug, we bent down to give Dorsey his. Mahoney took a dog bone from his jacket pocket which Dorsey accepted as his well-deserved reward while we told him what a good job he'd done.

"He's not the only one who did a good job," Molly said as she hurried over to us. "Did you hear that audience?"

Eileen and Arlene ran up.

"You were fabulous!"

"I don't know how you did it! I was so afraid when we couldn't find your notes."

Mahoney raised his eyebrows in a question, but didn't say anything.

The stage manager came over. "We've got a traffic jam in the lobby with people milling around waiting to meet you. Will you go up there?"

I glanced at Mahoney. "Go. You can't afford to offend your fans."

"I'll go if you two will come with me."

Mahoney handed Dorsey's leash to me. "You two go."

Molly placed her hand on Mahoney's arm. "You might want to go with her. We had some trouble before the show, and she might need you up there."

Mahoney took back the leash in one hand and offered me his other arm. "Let's go."

Chapter 8

Mahoney and I had invited Eileen and Bill, Molly and Bert, and Arlene and Arty back to our house after the event for the equivalent of a cast party. We were hours later than expected because of all the people who wanted to meet me after the show. We sat around the great room sipping champagne and munching on finger food that Mahoney had prepared. It was good to sit and relax. Even my exuberant Dorsey curled up quietly by the couch. He was worn out from shaking paws and woofing his thanks to attendees who wanted to meet him too.

"We don't have a final count yet, but we raised a ton of money," Molly said. "All those ticket sales! The house was full with standing room only for those who came at the last minute."

"And the bake sale! We had so many ladies baking, I was sure we'd have a lot left over," said Eileen. "But there were only five cupcakes and two packages of cookies left."

"It helped that everyone wanted to stick around and meet you. Buying goodies gave them something to do while they waited," Arlene added.

"The 50-50 sale brought in a couple of thousand."

"And the donation box was full. A lot of small change, but who cares? It was a big jar."

"Don't forget the big companies who made special

contributions," Arlene said. "We're got a dozen checks ranging from $500 to $1,000 each."

Molly gave me a hug. "And it's all thanks to you."

"Oh, no, you don't! It's thanks to us and all those volunteers and the people who bought tickets. I'd say a community effort at its best. Everyone contributed in some way."

"Amen to that," said Bill. "Captain says police morale has never been higher from the Chief down to the patrolmen. And Officer Blakely and his family? They're almost in shock at the support from the community."

"Speaking of that, you four girls know that you're in for a command performance, don't you?" asked Arty.

"What are you talking about?"

"There'll be a 'to do' when the Chief presents the check to the family. Press, the brass, the whole show. And he wants you girls there."

"But we asked him to present the check because that's exactly what we didn't want."

"Oh, well, that's what you get for being heroes."

"Do we have to say anything?"

"Not if you don't want to."

"One of us should," I said, "to make sure the community knows that we aren't taking all the credit, but representing them. Just a quick thanks to the organizers, the volunteers, and the people who attended, that sort of thing."

"You're the public speaker," Eileen said. "Would you do it?"

"I don't think it should be me. I didn't work with the organizers and the volunteers. Besides, I pushed my luck speaking without my notes; let's not tempt fate."

Mahoney leaned forward. "Yeah, what was that all about?"

"She left her notes on the stage manager's table while the tech checked her makeup. Someone stole them," Molly said.

"Don't forget about removing the orange cones," Arlene added, "so she wouldn't have a parking space."

"Sounds like sabotage," said Bert.

"Any idea who it might be?" asked Mahoney.

We girls exchanged glances. I turned to Molly.

"Did you ever find out why Bethany was backstage?"

Mahoney sat up straighter in his chair. I had finally told him about my run-ins with Bethany.

"At the last minute she asked one of the volunteers selling 50-50 tickets if they could exchange jobs. The volunteer didn't see any reason not to."

"So Bethany was free to roam around wherever she wanted to?" Mahoney asked.

"Yes."

"Did she have a reason to be backstage?"

"Volunteers selling 50-50 tickets were told to stay out front with the crowd," Molly answered. "People backstage were too busy to be buying tickets. So I know of no reason for her to be back there."

"And who saw her backstage?"

"Molly and I did. That's when I asked Molly what she was doing back there."

"Eileen and I saw her too," Arlene said.

"When did you see her backstage?" Mahoney asked.

I paused, thinking. "Just before we discovered the notes missing. We were walking back from the dressing room to the wings when we caught a glimpse of her. Then we got to the stage manager's table, and the notes were gone."

"You said a 'glimpse.' Are you sure it was her?"

"It's rather hard to mistake her, the way she dresses."

"We were a bit behind the others. She rushed right past us," said Eileen.

"Let's go back to the parking space and the orange cones. Would Bethany have been in the vicinity when someone removed them?"

"She should have been," Molly said. "The 50-50 volunteers were asked to be in place at least a half-hour before the show. I saw the cones in place when I went out to check that at least some of them were."

"Bert," Mahoney said, "I'm going to have a little chat with Bethany. Want to come along?"

"Sure do," Bert answered.

Chapter 9

How I wish I could have been there when Mahoney and Bert interviewed Bethany! But, alas, I had to be content with Mahoney's retelling of it after the fact.

They chose to interview her at work. When they told the car dealership owner that they'd like to talk with Bethany, he offered to step out and let them use his office. Mahoney told him they'd prefer it if he stayed with them.

Mahoney and Bert had to be careful. They had no real evidence that Bethany had tried to sabotage my talk or that she'd been the one to use my address, or give it to someone else to use. And there was that nagging little fact that the description of the person who bought the bracelet sent to me did not match Bethany's. Who could forget her ostentatious manner of dressing?

When Bethany came in, they explained that they'd like her help with some general information. Miss Helpful was all smiles. Mahoney and Bert resorted to basic detective tactics: get a statement first; poke holes in it afterward. When people try to change their statements, it doesn't look good for them.

They began by asking her if she had ever used or shared confidential information from a customer's paperwork. On their first visit to the dealership, they had only interviewed the owner, not Bethany, and wanted her official denial. She insisted she had not. They then asked the owner to confirm the penalties for violating that confidentiality. Bethany squirmed a little in her seat. Mahoney and Bert noted her reaction but did not press the issue. They had no proof that she had used or given out my address, but just asking her the question might also put the owner on alert.

Mahoney and Bert moved on to the night of the Blakely event. They asked her to explain her job that night, where she'd been stationed, and when she'd arrived. More confident again once they moved away from first subject, Bethany told them she'd worked as a 50-50 volunteer. Her job was in the front of the auditorium by the doors and in the lobby, and that she'd arrived about 30 minutes before the start of the show. Had she seen anyone removing the orange cones that reserved my parking space? No, she hadn't paid any attention to parking spaces, and she'd stayed in the lobby, not outside. Had she been backstage that night? No, she'd been too busy out front selling tickets.

Now came the fun, at least for Mahoney and Bert. Hadn't her original job been a ticket- taker? Well, yes. Why change? She didn't want to be stuck in one spot. Had she asked the organizers, or at least told them, about changing her job? Well, no. So with her new job, she was free to roam around? Yes.

Mahoney pretended to look at his notes. The orange cones were removed less than half an hour before the show, and according to his notes, she had been there and free to wander in the vicinity of the parking space. Was that correct? She stumbled through maybe, I guess, she didn't really know. You don't know where you were? Well, out front, but she wasn't sure exactly where; it wasn't like she stayed in one spot. Bethany wasn't smiling anymore.

And you were out front the whole time? Yes. You didn't go backstage? No. At least half a dozen witnesses had seen her backstage. How could she explain that? They must be mistaken. Oh, no, she forgot. She did go backstage for a few minutes to see if anyone wanted to buy tickets. When was that? Oh, about 10 or 15 minutes before the show.

Bert referred to his notes. That was about the time someone stole my notes. Had she seen anyone around the stage manager's table? No. By now, Bethany kept her head down and answered in whispers.

Lastly, Mahoney brought up my run-ins with her. She didn't know what he was talking about. I was lying; they didn't happen. She folded and unfolded her hands or picked at unseen lint on her skirt.

Mahoney returned to the implication she might have broken the dealership's confidentiality rule. Had she ever seen my paperwork? She didn't recall. Bert asked the owner if she might have seen my paperwork. Of course, she had. She computerized all the paperwork. That was her job.

No concrete proof, but the circumstantial evidence formed a mountain range. Mahoney and Bert knew it, Bethany knew it, and so did her boss. Mahoney and Bert thanked the owner and left. Guess I'll never know what happened in the office after that between Bethany and her boss. Darn.

Chapter 10

The Chief of Police held his press conference a week after the event for Officer Blakely. Molly had agreed to speak for us if I'd help her write what to say. No problem there. The press conference was held outside on the lawn in front of the police station. I don't normally attend such conferences so I didn't realize the large number of attendees was very unusual until Eileen whispered, "Wow! I've never seen so many people at a press conference."

The Chief began. "I don't think I have ever seen a community stand so solidly behind its police. I want to thank each and every person who contributed to this event. Whether you bought a ticket, or baked a cake, or made a donation, together you have made a huge difference for Officer Blakely and his family. But there are four special women standing here beside me who made this all happen."

As the Chief spoke, Molly nudged me. "There's Bethany, over to your right." Of course, once she said that I had to glance over. Bethany stood on the sideline pouting with her arms folded across her chest.

"I would like to introduce them." The Chief acknowledged us one by one. When he finished, Molly stepped up to the mike. She reiterated what the Chief had said about this being a community event and gave special thanks to the organizers and volunteers. "But no matter how hard we all worked, this event could not have taken place without one special person." Oh, oh, I thought, I didn't write this part of her address. "And that, of course, is one of the newer members of our community." Molly indicated me with a wave of her hand. Eileen and Arlene stepped back so I stood by myself. "Let's thank her and welcome her to Cedar Falls." The attendees applauded.

"Look at Bethany," Eileen whispered. Bethany stood staring at us, her body rigid, her hands clenched at her sides, and her face bright red. She spun around and stomped off.

The Chief took the mike back. "Officer Blakely cannot be with us today. His progress is good, I'm happy to report, but his attending was out of the question. I would like to introduce you to his wife. Mrs. Blakely." The Chief held his hand out to her.

Mrs. Blakely stepped up to the mike to join him. "On behalf of the community, I would like to present this check to you for..." When he mentioned the amount, the attendees burst out in loud applause with a few cheers and whistles thrown in.

Mrs. Blakely accepted the check with trembling hands. "I...I..." From where we stood, we could see her eyes fill with tears. "Thank you," she managed to say in a shaky voice. Another round of loud applause.

A couple of days later, Mahoney sat at the kitchen island drinking coffee and reading the morning paper while I played with Dorsey and Charlie on the floor. Dorsey keeps trying to teach her to play ball with him, but Charlie is only interested in batting it and chasing it herself, so I play referee. I heard Mahoney sputter and looked up. "Are you okay?" I asked.

He wiped his mouth. "Fine."

The tight line of his mouth, however, indicated anger, not 'fine.' I left the cat and dog to work things out for themselves to join Mahoney at the island. He quickly shut the newspaper.

"Mahoney?"

"It's nothing."

"You don't get angry over 'nothing'." I stretched my arm out to pick up the newspaper.

He stopped my reach in mid-air. "Don't. Please."

"So it's about me." Since the successful event for Blakely, I'd gotten quite a bit of coverage in the press. "Mahoney, not everyone thinks I'm great and wonderful. The only way I can deal with the negative is to know what it is."

"You really won't like it."

"All the more reason to know what it is. Please show me."

Mahoney shrugged, opened the paper to the editorial page, and pointed to a letter to the editor.

Dear Editor,

I am very upset about the praise you are giving to some people in this town, especially that writer who took all of the credit for raising money for Officer Blakely. What about all the other people who worked the event? If she is so wonderful, why is she living with her boyfriend? Many people consider that sinful. She should be ashamed. Our children need positive role models, not someone who takes advantage of a guy to support her. And have you even read those books of hers? They're as bad as she is. She should pack up and leave Cedar Falls and go back to wherever she came from. We don't need people like her.

B. Witherspoon

It took one phone call from Mahoney to confirm that the B. Witherspoon was indeed Bethany. For the most part, I've learned to control my Irish temper, but not that morning. I paced up and down the great room floor. "Took all of the credit?" Pace, pace. Turn. "How could she..." Pace, pace. Turn. "What did she think..." Pace, pace. Turn.

Mahoney stood nearby with his arms folded over his chest. He let me vent without interrupting.

I flung my arms in the air. "If I'm living in sin..."

Finally Mahoney spoke. "I know how to stop that kind of talk once and for all."

"Sure. Arrest her." Pace, pace. Turn. "For what?" Pace, pace. Turn. "How can you stop it?"

"Marry me."

"Right. Marr..." I stopped dead in my tracks and spun around to face him. "Marr...marry you?"

Mahoney unfolded his arms and held them out to me. "It would solve the problem of your 'living in sin,' wouldn't it?"

"Oh, Mahoney." I went to him and let him hold me for a minute. Only a minute. I was still boiling. I backed away from him. "Mahoney, I love you. I love living here with you." I spread my arms in an arc. "I love everything about my life. I'm happy. You've given me so much. But that doesn't mean you should have to marry me just because that b..." I was ready to start pacing again.

Mahoney caught my arm and pulled me to him. "You're right. I don't *have* to marry you. I *want* to marry you. I've *wanted* to marry you for a long time. Everything between us happened so quickly, and you had so much to handle after everything you went through. I didn't want to push it. I wanted to give you time to adjust before I asked you."

He pushed me back so he could look into my eyes. "You know I love you, don't you?"

I nodded.

"You said I've given you so much. Don't you think you've

given me just as much?"

Had I? He was sharing his house with me. I thought about his welcoming Charlie and Dorsey along with me. I thought about lots of little things: his lending me his car before I replaced mine, his...

Mahoney's a detective; he's a mind reader. "Stop making lists in your head. Get to the bottom line. Can you think of one reason why you shouldn't marry me?"

I looked up at him with watery eyes. "No."

"Okay, so let's try this again. Will you marry me?"

I flung my arms around him. "Yes, Mahoney, yes."

We sealed our agreement with a kiss, a very long one.

"Oh, I'm forgetting something. Wait here." He disappeared into the bedroom. When he reemerged, he held something clutched in his hand. He opened his hand to display a small jewelry box and pulled the lid open. Inside lay a ring with a rather large diamond that glittered in the light.

"I told you I've been *wanting* to ask you for a long time."

He took the ring out of the box and slipped it on my finger. I held up my hand, as women do, to admire it.

"You haven't said a word," Mahoney said. "You like it, don't you?"

I put my hand on his cheek. "Mahoney, it is the most beautiful thing I've ever seen, aside from you, that is."

Chapter 11

Bethany's letter started a mini-war in town. The newspaper was so inundated by replies, that they apologized for not being able to print them all. Instead, they printed a few letters representing the general sentiment from the flood of responses and summarized the rest in an article with quotations from readers.

The article included quotes such as "What century is B. Witherspoon living in?" or "Does she know it takes two to tango? Why doesn't she condemn the boyfriend too?"

"If she's so worried about role models, why not attack those sports players and politicians with their scandalous affairs. They're the real role models who create a negative impact." Well, okay, that was a bit of a put-down.

"Obvious she's never read those wonderful books." Thanks, reader!

One person said she knew B. Witherspoon and had been working with Bethany on her paperwork at the car dealership, but had canceled her order for a new car. "If that's the kind of people they hire, I don't want to deal with them."

A lawyer offered his services for free if I wanted to sue for libel.

The newspaper's selection of complete letters to print included a letter that stressed no one individual had taken credit for the event, that everyone at the conference emphasized it had been a community event. Perhaps the writer should have her hearing checked.

The newspaper also printed the complete letters from the Mayor and from the Chief of Police. Both praised me—and the other girls—for our community service and pointed out that our personal lives had nothing to do with our efforts to help Officer Blakely and his family. Go team!

Bethany's attack on me had backfired big time. Not only did I feel vindicated, but I held up my hand and admired my twinkling diamond. In the end, she'd brought me joy. Not so for her. When a reader had brought in her connection to the car dealership, the owner fired her. She had already been skating on thin ice after Mahoney and Bert's interview, and once her actions invoked the ire of the community toward his business, he couldn't afford to keep her. I almost felt sorry for her—almost.

The next edition of the newspaper contained a lone letter to the editor in support of Bethany.

"Doesn't she have the right to express her opinion? Isn't it guaranteed by the Fifth Amendment?" No, dummy, it isn't. That's the First Amendment you're referring to. The letter was signed E. Handley.

Newspapers only print the name, or a partial name depending on their policy, with a letter to the editor but require that the person submitting a letter to the editor include a full name, address, and phone number. That's for legal reasons.

Freedom of speech is guaranteed by the First Amendment—get that E. Handley—but that doesn't mean someone else can't object to what you say. Should a legal dispute arise over the contents, it is the writer of the letter, not the newspaper, which is ultimately held responsible. As a common expression goes, "Be prepared to put your money where your mouth is."

I didn't know it at the time, but after a call from the police to the newspaper editor, Mahoney had all the information about the writer of the letter tucked away in his files. It would come in handy later.

Chapter 12

Mahoney and I got down to the nitty-gritty of wedding plans. There was no reason to wait, and we decided the sooner, the better.

"Are you sure you don't want one of those big formal weddings?" Mahoney asked.

"I'm sure."

Mahoney looked relieved. "But I'm not running away to Vegas or one of those places to get married."

"Me either," I said. "If you want to do that, you'll have to go by yourself."

"So what are you thinking?"

"A simple ceremony somewhere around here followed by a simple reception. No rubber-chicken dinners either. Hors-d'oeuvres, finger food, a cake, that kind of thing."

"I'm with you on that. We could have the reception here. I could make..."

"Mahoney, you are *not* playing chef on our wedding day."

He grinned. "Okay, I suppose I could let someone else in my kitchen for one day. We could have it catered."

"I don't want the reception here. Too much work before and after. Besides, it would be awkward when it's time for us to leave—you know, for the honeymoon."

"Why? What difference does that make if we're leaving?"

"Because we're going to spend our first night as Mr. and

Mrs. right here. We can't leave if we're not going anywhere."

He looked surprised. "You don't want a honeymoon?"

"I want a honeymoon. I can't wait for the two of us to be together without any distractions. But I want to spend the first night here."

"That's okay with me, but why?"

"A wedding day is supposed to be the 'happiest day in a girl's life,' right?"

"I guess."

"Well, I want to end that day in a place where I'm happiest. And that's right here, not some strange hotel room."

He reached over and took my hand. "I love you." So much said in those three little words.

"We can leave on our honeymoon the next day."

"Where do you want to go?"

The practical side of me is never too far away. "That might depend on how long you can get off work. Do you have any place in mind?"

"Not really. Just someplace not too busy. Like that inn we stayed in after we caught the twins. I don't mean the same inn. Just something like it."

"We'll do some Internet searches."

"We haven't gotten very far on making decisions."

"Sure we have. We've agreed on what kind of wedding and honeymoon we want, haven't we?"

"But not where."

"That's the easier part, now that we know what we want. Although we will have to make a list of who we want to invite so we'll know how many people before we go traipsing around looking at reception places."

He slumped back in his chair. "I didn't think about having to do all that."

"So how's this? You go off catching the bad guys, and the girls and I will do the traipsing. They'll love it. We'll narrow the possibilities down to two or three, and you'll only have to look at those."

"You wouldn't mind that?"

"Not at all. I want all the bad guys in jail before the wedding so you won't have to think about them during our honeymoon."

He laughed. "Wouldn't that be nice!"

Chapter 13

"Speaking of bad guys, Mahoney, how's the investigation going on the shooting? Still pursuing our, oh excuse me, *your* theory about the robbers being mutes?"

Mahoney poured the sauce he'd mixed into a pan. "Slow going on that. Standstill is more like it. We're not getting much cooperation from the mute community. There's a sign language school a couple of miles out of town. The Sign Language Center. Many of the deaf and the mute associate with that school in one way or another.

"A couple of the guys went out there, but it was a waste of time. They think we're accusing them all of something or profiling. And without any evidence, we can't get a court order forcing them to talk...oops, wrong words...forcing them to cooperate. That reminds me. I brought something home to show you. There's a piece of paper in my jacket pocket. Would you get it?"

I retrieved the paper and read it as I returned to the kitchen.

Don't say anything; keep hands where I can see them. Put money on the bag. Immediately.

"What's this?"

"That's a copy of the note the robbers gave to the tellers. Same note to all the tellers. So what do *I* think about it?"

"For one, it could be looked at as a confirmation of the

mute theory. For two, *you* think it shows that the writer is educated and a foreigner."

Mahoney stopped stirring the pot with the sauce for our dinner, put the spoon down, and joined me at the kitchen island.

"And why do *I* think that?"

"Look at the first sentence. *Don't say anything.* Why should the robber care? Because if the teller asks a question, he can't answer. Better not to face that situation. *...keep hands where I can see them.* That's somewhat standard. *You* assume that's so the teller can't push a panic button or go for a gun, right?"

Mahoney nodded.

"But look what joins those two sentences together—a semi-colon. Most people don't know how to use a semi-colon. But it's used correctly here. Hence, *you* assume the writer is educated. Now jump to the last part, *Immediately.* Would you expect a robber to use a twenty-five cent word?"

"No. Most of them would stop at 'Put the money in the bag,' or say 'right now' or something similar."

"Exactly. It's an odd choice of words and one that indicates a good vocabulary. Now look at *Put money on the bag.* That's why *you* think he's foreign. When you repeated the phrase a minute ago, you said 'Put the money in the bag,' which is what a native speaker would say. Articles and prepositions are the hardest to learn in a foreign language because we learn them more from hearing than from rules."

"Explain."

"Okay, so we might say 'Money is the root of all evil.' No article in front of 'money.' Or we might say 'Do you have money?' or 'Do you have any money?' If we say 'Do you have the money?' the meaning changes slightly. Those nuisances are hard for a non-native speaker."

Mahoney pointed back to the first sentence. "Isn't that the same thing here when it says 'keep hands' instead of 'keep your hands'?"

"Exactly. And the 'on the bag' instead of 'in the bag.' Take the preposition 'dans' in French. It can be translated as 'in, into, out of, from, among, or about.' It all depends on the context. Choosing the wrong preposition as the note writer did is a common type of error for non-native speakers."

"Hey, I'm pretty smart, aren't I?"

"Yah, but not such a good chef tonight. Your dinner is burning."

"Damn." Mahoney grabbed the pot off the stovetop.

Mahoney salvaged the sauce, and we continued the conversation during dinner.

"A mute and a foreigner, or a foreign born American, narrows down the possibilities. But if we can't get the mute community to talk...there I go again...cooperate with us, it's difficult to follow up on the theory."

"Hmmm. Maybe I can do that for you."

"You gonna borrow my badge?"

"No, I'll be me—a writer."

"And?"

"What if I contacted them and said I was planning to include a mute character in one of my books? That I wanted a better understanding of the difficulties they face so I could be more sensitive to their problems. If there's any certain ways a mute character might react in a given situation. Might a situation be dangerous if a character couldn't speak? That kind of thing. If you guys give me a list of the questions you'd like to ask, I could try to create a character or situations that might elicit the responses you're looking for."

"And in the meantime be looking around the place."

"Bet I can get them to give me a tour."

Mahoney sat back in his chair and stopped eating. "That might work."

"It's a way in that you don't have now."

"I'll run it by Palmer. The first question he'll have is about your safety going undercover for us."

"What undercover? I'm a writer doing research. Hopefully someone there will be familiar with my books. I'm me and I'm going as me."

"Did I ever tell you I love you?"

"Yes, but you can tell me again."

"You won't be nervous or..."

"Mahoney, I interview people all the time, or at least I used to. I've been off my game, and it's time to reclaim my life as a writer. I might actually enjoy this."

"I love you."

Chapter 14

I practically floated into the restaurant the next day for lunch with the girls. I hadn't seen them since the press conference. I kept my left hand tucked under the sweater I carried. As I walked to the table, I heard them whispering.

"She didn't see it."

"I hope not."

"Oh, I saw it," I said. "If you mean that letter to the editor."

"You're not upset?"

"Upset doesn't cover it. I was spitting mad. Ask Mahoney. Poor guy, he had to listen to my tirade."

"You look radiant today. What changed?"

"This." I held out my left hand.

The girls jumped out of their chairs to admire the ring up close and congratulate me. Oh, yeah, and a few hugs thrown in. After we settled back down at the table, they wanted the details: when and where.

"There's where you guys come in," I said. "I need your help."

"Anything."

"What can we do?"

"Ask away."

"You know I'm not very familiar with places in town where we could host the reception. I need your suggestions.

Then I'm hoping you'll come with me to check them out. I figured we could narrow the possibilities down to two or three, before I take Mahoney to look at them."

"What fun!"

"Count on it!"

"Let's start brainstorming right now."

The girls and I met several days later to check out locations on our brainstorming list. Most had cavernous rooms for our small group, and the owners proudly supplied us with samples menus of full-course dinners. No thanks. Maybe Mahoney and I should run away to Vegas.

Sensing my frustration, Arlene suggested a location not on our list. "There's a new restaurant on the outskirts of town. I don't know a lot about it, but a few people I've talked to raved about the food." She checked her watch. "We're past due for lunch anyway. Let's go there for lunch, taste the food, and see what it's like at the same time."

We pulled up to the restaurant, the Cedar Inn. Rustic instead of formal. Trees for neighbors instead of other buildings. Ample parking. "I like," I said as I stepped out of the car.

We decided to eat first. If the food wasn't good, why bother asking about a banquet room? We ordered different dishes and shared them. Eileen, who likes to cook and makes the world's best deviled eggs, said, "They're all really good." We agreed.

"Okay," I said, "it's passed two tests. Now for the third."

We asked to speak with the manager. The owner himself joined us. "What can I do for you ladies?"

I explained that I was looking for a place to hold my wedding reception and what I wanted in terms of a room and menu. He beamed. "Please, let me show you the facilities first."

He took us back to a large dining room. Plenty of space for our group without being too big. Several large windows overlooked the restaurant's backyard. A flat lawn swept down to the tree line. Not another building in sight. "Oh, it's lovely!"

"Thinking of the wedding ceremony?" Arlene asked.

"Yes."

While we examined the room, Mark, that's the owner, had excused himself to get some menus. He handed me a list of possible hors d'oeuvres and finger food. This was Mahoney's department.

"As for a wedding cake, we can make one for you, or you can have one delivered. Whichever you prefer." I liked his non-pushy approach.

"If you would pick out your top choices, we'll make up samples, and you ladies could come back and try them before making a final decision."

"I'd really like that," I said, "but I'll bring my fiancé with me." Heaven forbid I should make decisions about food without my chef at my side.

Mark gave me his card, and I promised I'd call to set up an appointment. I did a little dance on the way back to the car. "I think she likes it," Eileen said. The others laughed.

When Mahoney and I returned to sample the hors d'oeuvres and finger food, they received his approval. Phew! He even decided we should stay for dinner—that was more than just approval. And he liked the facilities as much as I did. We stood in front of one of the windows overlooking the back lawn.

"You know, Princess, that would be a great place for the ceremony."

The owner overheard us. "We'd be happy to set up for the ceremony as well."

"Done," said Mahoney. "Oh, sorry." Mahoney turned to me. "I shouldn't have said that without your..."

"Done," I said.

Mark happily went off to draw up a contract while we ate dinner. Two big items checked off the 'to do' list.

Since Eileen and Arlene both work part-time, only Molly joined me to shop for the other two biggies on the 'to do' list: a dress for me and invitations. First stop, a local bridal shop. We sifted through rack after rack of dresses, all with ruffles or lace or long flowing trains. Too formal and not me at all!

"There's another bridal shop on..."

"Forget it," I said. "They'll have the same type of assortment. What this tells me is that I don't want a bridal gown; I want a simple white dress."

"Department store or boutique type shopping?"

"Exactly." We left the bridal shop.

"Before we leave here, there's a specialty card shop just down there." She pointed down the street. "Let's look at the invitations."

Once again we ran into 'formal.' Fancy inserts for the reception and for the can/can't attend with little envelopes. Oh, and don't forget the six weeks in advance to order them. They'd get here after the wedding. I closed the book I'd been rifling through. "Molly, how would Derek like a job—a paying one this time?"

"He'd be thrilled."

That took care of the invitations. A visit to a couple of dress shops took care of my dress. Mahoney had arranged for a photographer through a friend of his, and with a quick visit to a florist, I ordered flowers. All the 'biggies' crossed off the list.

Chapter 15

While preparations for the wedding continued, Mahoney told me Lieutenant Palmer had okayed a visit to the Sign Language Center. Of course, he didn't really have any jurisdiction to stop me, but I felt better going with his blessing, and I needed the cooperation of the department to ensure my visit would be fruitful for them. I wrote a business letter to Mrs. Higgins, the director of the school, introducing myself and asking if she would help me with my research.

She replied quickly. They would be delighted to assist me, and would I have time for a tour of the school while I was there to get a full picture of the scope of what they do? She also mentioned that they had several of my books in their school library, and when funding permitted, would complete the set because the books were popular with both students and staff.

I don't know if that was a hint or not, but I figured it was a fair exchange. Since my extra copies of my books had burned along with everything else, I called my publisher and asked him to send a complete set of my books to the school a.s.a.p. Oh, yes, and a set for me too. I chose a date from the ones Mrs. Higgins suggested and set up the appointment.

Palmer arranged a meeting with an agent from the FBI and all the detectives involved in the case, including

Mahoney. Under normal circumstances, they may not have been as open with a civilian, but because of my connection to Mahoney and our event for Blakely, they were willing to listen to me. Okay, so the FBI rep wasn't fond of the idea and was more reserved than the others.

With their input in mind, I sat down at the computer to create a scenario and a fictitious character. I liked the result. I might actually use this in a future novel. Mahoney checked over my work and tweaked it in a few places. He knows the real bad boys so I readily accepted his revisions. I saved the file and closed it for a future day.

I was checking my email while Mahoney cooked. "Mahoney, we're got a problem."

He put down the spatula and looked up at me. "What's that?"

"Wedding presents."

"Huh?"

"Wedding presents. The girls want to know if we have a wish list. I haven't given a thought to presents. Have you?"

"No. Do we need presents?"

"No. But they're going to buy them anyway, and it might be better if we gave people some idea of what we want."

"Give me a little time to think about it."

When I woke up the next morning, Mahoney lay on his back staring up at the ceiling with his hand under his head. Usually he gives me a good morning kiss, but he didn't move.

"Hey, you."

He put an arm around me, but kept staring at the ceiling. "I've been thinking."

"About?"

"Wedding presents."

"And?"

He rolled over to face me.

"Do we have to ask for traditional presents? Like dishes or glasses or stuff like that?"

"No. A lot of people now ask for money toward something like their honeymoon, or for people to pay for some activity to enjoy on the honeymoon like a special dinner or massages…"

"I don't want money."

"So what are you thinking?"

He ran his hand up and down my arm.

"This may sound weird. You know I want to finish that office… I could use some help, some man-hours. What if we asked the guys to donate some time to help me as their present?"

"Do they have the skills?"

"Most of my friends have skills of some sort—some with a hammer, some with a paint brush."

"They can't build and paint at the same time."

"Hmmm." He rolled away to stare at the ceiling again. "What if we had two crews? One to help with the building and one to help with the finishing."

"That might work."

He turned to face me again.

"You wouldn't feel cheated out of having presents?"

"Are you kidding? What better present could I ask for than to have my office finished?"

"So you like the idea?"

"I do. We need to think about the women though. They need to be included or they'll just go shopping for something on top of that…I know! We'll ask the women to bring food to feed all you hungry guys. Like an old-fashioned barn-raising."

"I like it."

"I do worry about one thing. I don't want to be sitting at my desk and have the roof fall on top of me. How do we know it'll all be done correctly?"

"I thought of that. I worked with a contractor when I built the frame. I could hire him as a supervisor to give directions, double-check the work, etc. I'll also ask him to handle the electrical and heating so we have experts doing that." He leaned over and kissed my forehead. "I certainly don't want the roof falling on your pretty little head. How do we tell them?"

"I'll make up a...No, I'll ask Derek to create an insert we can put in with the invitations so they go together."

I finally got my morning kiss.

Chapter 16

Mahoney and I had two big events before *the* big event. One, the first office 'barn-raising' to complete the outside structure. Two, my appointment at the sign language school.

Derek had done a marvelous job on the invitations and inserts. No syrupy little flowers or wedding rings or traditional sayings.

Mahoney is tenacious once he makes a decision, and as he said, he'd put off finishing the extra room long enough. He didn't add that was because of me and all the personal time he'd dedicated to my case. So we'd set the date for the first office 'barn-raising' before the wedding and the second for after the wedding.

The replies came in fairly evenly divided between the guys who wanted to work on the outside construction and those who wanted to work on the finishing. Mahoney said they thought the idea for the wedding present a 'hoot.' Of course that also evenly divided the number of women bringing food. How convenient! I organized the 'who brings what' so we didn't end up with all potato salads. Organizing food I can do; it's the cooking of it that stymies me.

On the invitation to Pete and Jennie DeLane, I added a note asking if they would take care of Charlie and Dorsey while we went on our honeymoon instead of attending an office 'barn-raising.' Jennie replied that they would be delighted to take the kids—what's a couple of extra animals on a farm? But in no way would they miss an office 'barn-raising.' They signed up for the construction crew.

The first 'barn-raising' went well. The guys arrived early in the morning and hoisted piece after piece of lumber from the piles at the top of the driveway over to the walls to nail up. Dorsey joined in to help and grabbed lumber in his mouth to drag over for them. Mahoney grabbed his harness and shouted to me, "The house or his leash."

Into the house we went until the wives arrived. We'd set up the eating area in front of the house, well away from the construction area. Dorsey was content on his leash as we set the tables with food—until he figured out he wasn't going to get any. Then he stretched the leash as far as possible toward the construction and barked. "Mom, let me go. I belong with the guys!" He changed his mind when Arlene appeared with her yorkies, Elvis and Zorro. We tethered all three dogs around a tree and let them play.

After the men ate and resumed working, we women leisurely sat around and chatted. They decided our idea for a wedding present was a 'hoot' too. In time, the hammers stopped banging, the women packed up the left-overs, and cars departed. Mahoney and I thanked everyone and waved as they left.

"So what'd ya think, Princess?"

We stood side by side gazing at the top of the drive. Instead of piles of lumber and roofing materials blocking the driveway, the two-by four skeleton had transformed into an addition to the house.

"It looks so different! I want to see the inside."

We unleashed Dorsey, walked around to the back, and entered through the French doors.

"Look how big it is!" I said. Light poured through the

windows. "And bright!" I hugged him. "Thank you, thank you."

"You sure you want to be doing that right now?"

I sniffed. "You have a point."

Mahoney arranged for the contractor to wire the room for the electric and heating midway between the two 'barn-raisings,' while we were on our honeymoon. I must admit I wouldn't miss the noise and mess. Charlie wouldn't have to hide all day—she doesn't like noisy men, and I wouldn't have to fight again with Dorsey who'd naturally want to supervise and get under-foot. All Mahoney and I had to do for that phase of it was indicate where we wanted outlets and switches. We added plenty to cover all possibilities both inside the room and outside for the patio.

After Mahoney went to work on Monday, I picked up the newspaper he had left on the kitchen island. I discovered that there'd been another incident at 345 Summit. This time someone had broken into their car, put glue in the ignition lock, and smeared dog poo all over the inside. Yuck!

"Hey, Dorsey, want to go for a walk?" I wanted to see which house was being targeted.

Dorsey appeared at my side with his leash in his mouth. "I'm ready."

As we strolled down the street, I saw a tow truck pull into a driveway. Was that number 345? With glue in the ignition lock, they'd need a tow truck. I arrived at the house as the operator hoisted a car unto the lift. A quick glance at the mailbox confirmed it was 345. Two things hit me at the same time. This was the house where that man had slowed down and stared at me several weeks ago. And the car that the operator positioned for towing was the same make, model, and color as mine!

My mind whirled.

A voice broke my concentration. "May I help you?"

"Oh, sorry. I umm...I didn't mean to stare. It dawned on me that your car must be the one I read about in the newspaper. The one that was vandalized?"

"It is."

"I'm your neighbor. I live..."

"I know who you are, and I'm very pleased to meet you." We shook hands. "I attended your show and enjoyed every minute of it." He bent down to pet Dorsey. "And I'm pleased to meet you too." Dorsey offered his paw. The man laughed and shook it. "That's one incredible dog you have." I agreed.

"I'm Jim McGill. Alice, that's my wife, will never forgive me if I don't let her know you're here. Could you wait for a minute while I get her?" I did.

After introductions, the conversation shifted to his car. They were both very upset and had no idea who would do such a thing to them.

"Did you tell her about the note?" Alice asked Jim. Without waiting for an answer, she continued, "We found a note under the windshield wipers. The police took it, but I remember what it said. It said, 'Since the notes didn't upset you, maybe this will.' I can't imagine what that's supposed to mean."

Oh, oh, I knew. "That is very strange."

We chatted for a few more minutes and said goodbye. On the way home, I put the incidents together. The McGills had a car that looked like mine; the note left under the windshield referred to my notes stolen before the Blakely benefit.

I startled Dorsey when I stopped short. Their address was 345, mine 354. Someone had transposed the numbers! And don't forget that man who drove by and stared at me when I stood in the McGill's yard. Whoever it was thought I lived at the McGill's! Something else was nagging me about addresses, but what?

I stopped at the mailbox at the end of the driveway to pick up the mail. Mail! The post office returned the bracelet to Eileen because it had a wrong address, actually a wrong street number. I didn't recall the number on the package, but I bet I was 99.999% correct in guessing 345.

Now what didn't fit? A man had been driving the car. A woman other than Bethany had bought the bracelet. Had we been wrong in assuming Bethany's guilt in stealing my notes? But who other than Bethany had recently expressed animosity toward me? Or did she have an accomplice?

When I shared my suspicions later that evening with Mahoney, he assured me Bethany was involved somehow with the missing notes because of her reactions during the second interview at the dealership. And, yes, an accomplice, or accomplices, was entirely possible.

Chapter 17

The second big event before *the* big event was my appointment at the Sign Language Center. Mahoney reviewed my notes with me the night before and gave me some interviewing tips. Yes, yes, I'd done a lot of interviewing. But his were cop-interviewing techniques including looking for the slightest reactions. My arsenal for being a good interviewer was growing.

Mrs. Higgins came out of her office to meet me as soon as the receptionist announced my arrival. First, she thanked me for the donation of books. Good, they'd arrived. That set the tone for a friendly visit. She wanted to start with a tour of the school thinking that would present the best over-all picture and answer many of my questions along the way.

The school served deaf and mute students. Both needed sign language to communicate. Mrs. Higgins herself was deaf, but she read lips well as long as I faced her when I spoke. Sounds easy, huh? It was quite a lesson for me in how often we speak without directly facing someone by turning our backs or turning sideways or putting our heads down to look at something or holding something in front of our faces. Her speech was excellent with only a trace of the distorted sound characteristic of the deaf pronouncing words they'd never heard spoken.

My visit had obviously been announced to the school

beforehand. Wherever we stopped, students and teachers paused to welcome me, to answer questions, or to let me examine study materials. They even gave me a mini lesson on speaking in sign. I found the music room particularly fascinating as I watched the students convert vibrations into musical notes on their instruments.

A conversation, however, often required the effort of several people. For the deaf, an interpreter had to convert my question into sign before the person could answer. A mute person understood my question, but required an interpreter to convert his signed answer into words. Mrs. Higgins could have done this all herself, but she wanted to give her students an opportunity to interact with me. I'm glad she did.

I was so fascinated by all I was learning that I had to remind myself I was also here on a special mission. I didn't spot anything unusual until we visited the library.

In contrast to the rest of the school, the library suffered from age. Cramped quarters allowed only a couple of scarred tables for working, and tape held the upholstery on the chairs together. Old bookshelves sagged under the weight of the books. Carts stuffed with books crammed between the aisles of the stacks indicated a lack of space to house the collection properly. A student flipped through cards in an old card catalog, long ago replaced in most libraries with a computer.

Also in contrast to the people I'd met thus far, the librarian, Mr. Wong, went through the motions of welcoming me, but without a smile and without anything other than a formal bow. I got the impression that he felt I was intruding in his special domain. Okay, Mahoney, I'm paying attention.

Mrs. Higgins happily pointed out the window to the construction of a new building. They'd just received a gift to allow them to finally implement their plans for a new library. Okay, self, tread lightly. After congratulating them on this wonderful windfall, as casually as possible I asked when they received the gift and who it was from. I noticed Mr. Wong's body tighten slightly. Caught that, Mahoney. Mrs. Higgins said the gift arrived anonymously several weeks ago. And such a generous gift! She wished she knew who sent it because she wanted to thank them.

I turned to Mr. Wong and asked him how difficult it was going to be to move all those books. Wong signed to Mrs. Higgins. Deaf or mute? They signed back and forth several times. Unusual. The library door slammed shut. Mr. Wong turned toward the sound. Mute. He then bowed in my general direction and walked away.

Mrs. Higgins's genial expression turned to a frown. She apologized for his behavior, although never divulged what they'd said in that fast-paced sign conversation. I shrugged it off as though it wasn't important and asked a few more non-snoopy questions about the library. We took a few minutes to wander around before we left. I asked about an erasable board hanging on the wall. Mrs. Higgins said it was Wong's list of duties for his student volunteers. I memorized the few instructions.

We returned to Mrs. Higgins's office where she asked if I had any more questions. I asked a few of those I had initially prepared for the interview. I didn't really think they mattered now, but wanted to carry through my role as a researcher. I sincerely thanked her for her time and graciousness.

As soon as I got home, I rushed to the computer to make notes on my observations while they were fresh in my mind. Charlie and Dorsey sat off to my side. If animals could cross their arms and frown, they had. What's this? You're supposed to say hello to us first.

Chapter 18

I made up my ignoring Dorsey and Charlie by letting them outside. Charlie had totally acclimated to our new home and now considered outside the house her domain too. If she wandered too far away, Dorsey herded her back. I'd often assigned him the job of protecting her while I was gone, just to give him something to do. He now accepted that responsibility as part of his everyday duties.

While the kids played, I put on a pot of coffee for Mahoney and sat on the porch waiting for him. I couldn't wait to tell him what I'd discovered! I usually let him change clothes and relax with a cup of coffee before we discuss our days. Not today. When his car turned into the driveway, I ran inside, poured a cup of coffee for him, and met him on the porch with it. Dorsey ran around him with his usual 'Dad's home' welcome, and Charlie sat sedately on the porch steps for him to greet her. It's against cat rules to act too eager.

Mahoney made me repeat my story several times and added new questions with each repetition. Wong fit the profile we'd made up. Educated, mute, and most likely not American born. How did we know that? His Asian name? No, that might be a clue, but it was his instructions to his aides on the erasable board that we zeroed in on.

"Put returned books in cart." Instead of 'on the cart.'

"Dust shelves from bottom to top." Usually we say 'top to bottom.'

"File old magazines on bins." Those pesky prepositions again.

"Reshelf books resting on tables." 'Resting'? Not 'left'?

Okay, so it wasn't conclusive. It wasn't even enough to bring him in for questioning, but it was enough for the police to start digging into his past. Of course, this did not prove either that he had anything to do with the bank robbery, but the timing of the gift to the school fit the general time frame, and Mahoney's nose twitched at the coincidence.

He looked into his empty coffee cup and at an ink stain on his shirt. "How about I take a quick shower and change and we go out to dinner? I'd like to see if that new French place is any good."

I still wore my business attire for my day at the Sign Language Center. That's the advantage of versatile clothes. All I needed to do when we got to the restaurant is take off my jacket and I'd be wearing my sexy dress. I brought the kids in and fed them, so Mahoney and I were ready to go at the same time.

About an hour after Mahoney left for work the next morning, he phoned. "Can you make it down to the station in an hour?"

"Sure. What's up?"

Palmer called another meeting with all the guys assigned to this case and the FBI agent. He'd like our new ace detective to be there to give a firsthand report."

"Did he say 'our new ace detective'?"

"Not exactly."

At our second meeting, I went over the story again and answered questions. The detectives were all smiles. Even the FBI agent smiled. Whether my input led to something or not, at least they had new leads to follow. "I also have the opportunity to go back if you need me to. Mrs. Higgins asked if I'd be willing to speak informally with students interested in writing. I said I would, and she left it to me to determine when." Mahoney raised his eyebrow. I'd forgotten to tell him that.

"And Mahoney," Palmer said as the meeting broke up, "let Egger and Strong (that's Bert and Arty) take the lead on this for any public follow-up. I'd prefer you not be associated with the case for obvious reasons." He meant me.

I didn't go home right away. Molly and I had planned a window shopping trip to gather paint samples and look at office furniture. It was a bit early, but I headed to the paint store where we'd agreed to meet. By the time she called out a greeting, I had already chosen the color swatches. I wanted to paint the room a calm and soothing sage green.

On to the furniture stores. The plan was to browse so I'd know what was available. In store two, I wrote down the stock numbers of a desk and a comfortable chair I'd consider buying. It took longer to drive between the stores than walking through the stores themselves. Store four. Molly and I bent over a desk inspecting the drawers when a voice behind us hissed, "What are you doing here?"

We both straightened up and spun around. Bethany stood there with her hands on her hips, her face twisted into a sneer.

"Haven't you caused me enough trouble already? Are you here to get me fired from this job too?"

I love how miscreants so easily slip the responsibility for their actions around someone else. They, of course, never do anything wrong. I wanted to punch her in the face. Maybe more than wanted. Molly grabbed my arm and I noted my clenched fist.

"Go ahead," she said. "Hit me. I'd love to see another picture in the paper. This one of little Miss Perfect being arrested. Maybe then Jack will finally realize that his bride-to-be is..." She stopped. Her chest heaved.

Molly squeezed my arm. "Let's leave."

"Jack. My Jack. You turned him against me."

Her Jack? So many thoughts raced through my mind that I couldn't find words.

"You'll be sorry you did that."

Another salesman walked up. "Is there a problem here?"

Bethany turned all sweetness and smiles. "I asked them if I could help them, but she said no." The 'she' didn't come out so sweetly.

"She's right," I said, finally regaining my voice. "Nothing she does could possibly assist me."

The salesman swiveled his head back and forth between Bethany and me. Molly tugged at my arm and we walked away. We didn't stop until we reached the sidewalk.

"What did she mean by 'another picture'?"

I shrugged. "There's been a few because of the Blakely benefit. My question is how did she know we're getting married?"

"And what did she mean by you'll be sorry?"

Chapter 19

The answers to two of Molly's and my questions came soon afterward. Mahoney and I arrived home within fifteen minutes of each other. I read the newspaper while he went into change.

I turned a page and gasped. Mahoney and I did not want an announcement of our engagement or any news about the wedding in the newspaper. There in front of me was a picture of us under the headline "Engaged to be married." I scanned the brief story. It included the date of the wedding and named the Cedar Inn as the place for our reception.

"Mahoney!" I yelled, "Mahoney! What's this?" I don't yell very often; Mahoney came running.

"What's what?"

I pointed to the newspaper. He took it from me and read. "Damn."

"Where'd they get that picture?" Actually, I liked the photo. Not the standard posed headshots. Mahoney and I faced each other, laughing.

He looked closer. "The background looks like the interior of the high school auditorium."

That made sense. A lot of pictures were taken that night.

"What I'd like to know is where they got this info about the wedding." He glanced at the clock. "Too late to call now. I'll check in the morning."

We never did find out who called it in. I suppose it didn't make much of a difference. The info was already printed. My concern was Bethany. Obviously she'd seen it. I told Mahoney about my encounter with her in the furniture store.

"Her again?"

"Mahoney, did you ever date her?"

"No."

"Ever give her any reason to believe you were interested in her?"

Mahoney gave me a strange look. "I don't care if you did. I'm just trying to figure out why she called you 'my Jack'?"

"It's all in her head. Honestly. I don't even remember ever talking to her... before the interviews, that is. It's possible I did at some function or other, but if I did, it certainly wasn't anything personal. You believe me, don't you?"

"Of course I believe you. But you could do me one little favor."

"What's that?"

"Go put some pants on."

He looked down. I'd yelled while he was changing, and he'd come charging to the rescue in his skivvies. He laughed. "Then I suppose you want me to make dinner too?"

"I'll cook if you want." I'd tried twice. Twice was enough.

"Not in my kitchen you won't."

"Then I guess you're cooking."

While we ate, I asked him to catch me up on any developments in the bank robbery. Had my visit to the Sign Language Center helped them? Yes. Mr. Li Wong was foreign born. He'd been in this country for several years, all of them at the center. He'd answered an ad for the job as librarian.

"I guess the qualifications limited the number of

applicants. It had to be a trained librarian and someone fluent in sign with experience working with the deaf and mute."

I took another couple of bites of my pork chop. I don't know how he keeps them so moist. Mine are always so dry they're like chewing cardboard.

"He seems very dedicated to his job. He wrote a number of federal grants for funding for a new library, but didn't get them."

"You can trace what grants he wrote?"

Mahoney laughed. "The Feds never throw anything away. Private funding? We don't know if he tried for that."

"Frustrated and dedicated enough to find his own funding?"

"Could be. He lives off campus, here in town. We're nosing around neighbors to see if they've ever seen any of his visitors."

"In town... hmmm. That could explain where they disappeared to so quickly after the robbery. You're hoping the visitors might be his accomplices?"

Mahoney nodded. I'd caught him loading a forkful of mashed potatoes into his mouth.

"And the FBI is tracing the money trail to see where the 'gift' originated from."

Unfortunately, since Mrs. Higgins refused to cooperate with the police when they sought her assistance, she and the school also fell under suspicion when the press caught a whiff of the investigation into Wong. She refused to allow any interviews or give any comments. The press has a way of making uncooperative parties look guilty, as though they are hiding something, and the Blakely shooting was still an important news item in Cedar Falls. With few facts to report, the press resorted to innuendos.

Chapter 20

Our wedding was scheduled for Saturday. On Wednesday, Mark, the owner of the Cedar Inn called in an absolute panic.

"I don't know how I can do it! I have all the food for the hors d'oeuvres and finger sandwiches already ordered. And I'm not sure I can get..." The words rushed out of his mouth.

"Mark, slow down. Take a deep breath." I heard him inhale. "Okay, now tell me what the problem is."

"The changes you're making at the last minute! I don't know how..."

"Mark, stop. What changes?"

He sounded incredulous that I couldn't remember the changes I'd made.

"The ones you phoned in this morning! When you called to add two more dinners! When my assistant told you that we'd ordered enough hors d'oeuvres and finger food to easily accommodate two more people! When you said you'd changed your mind and now wanted full-course chicken dinners!"

"Mark, I haven't made any changes to the menu."

"When...what?"

I repeated. "I haven't made any changes to the menu."

It took him a few minutes to process that.

"This was a joke?" A sick prank described it better.

"It may have been someone's idea of a joke. Not mine, and obviously not yours."

"You didn't call?" He was catching on.

"No, Mark, I didn't call. And I'm very sorry someone has upset you like this." What about me?

"Everything's the same? No changes?"

"No changes. Everything is the same as we discussed: the ceremony, the reception."

"Oh, good." He sighed in relief. "But who would do such a terrible thing?"

"I don't know, Mark. But don't listen to any more phone callers claiming to be me. I can't imagine changing anything at this point, but if I have to discuss something with you, either Mahoney or I or both of us will come to see you in person, okay?"

When I said that, I never dreamed I'd created a problem for myself, nor did I think about what other changes someone may have made to my wedding plans.

Chapter 21

While I'd been waiting for Mahoney to come home, I turned on the news. The anchor was commentating on the headlines when he stopped and looked at his prompter.

"Ladies and gentlemen, we have a breaking news story. An officer has just been shot."

"Oh, no," I groaned, "not another one."

"Let us take you now to our reporter on the scene."

I recognized the rear of the police station in the background.

"Just a few minutes ago, a gunman opened fire on an officer exiting the police station."

She stepped aside to reveal chaos and a huddle of people surrounding paramedics as they lifted a gurney into an ambulance. I offered up a silent prayer for whoever it was.

"We have very few details at this moment and are awaiting confirmation of the victim's name and the seriousness of his injury."

Lieutenant Palmer stepped into view. The reporter rushed over to him and held up her mike.

"Lieutenant, can you tell us what happened and who's been shot?"

He ignored the first part of her question and answered the second.

"The victim is Detective Jack Mahoney..."

"Noooo," I screamed. My knees collapsed, and I landed on the floor. The TV screen became a blur and all sound ceased. Not Mahoney, no, it can't be; I heard it wrong. Okay, I calmed myself. Someone's been shot. You were waiting for Mahoney to come home, so he was on your mind, and you only thought you heard the lieutenant say his name.

My hearing slowly came back.

"...and can you tell us how serious his injuries are?"

"We won't know the full extent of his injuries until the doctors have had a chance to examine him, but any gunshot wound is serious."

Say a name again, but don't say Mahoney's...please?

A picture of Mahoney flashed on the screen. "Detective Jack Mahoney has been shot outside..."

My mind must have blanked out, but not my body. In my next conscious moment, I was standing by the front door holding a set of keys in my hand. "I have to get to Mahoney; I have to get to Mahoney. I have to get to the hospital; I have to get...

I couldn't get the key into the lock. How am I supposed to lock the door if I can't get the key in? I dropped my purse, and its contents scattered across the porch. Damn the door. I won't lock it. I bent over to gather my stuff and stick it back into my purse. Just get to the car...

I felt a hand gently touch my shoulder. I screamed. How had someone sneaked up on me like that? I jumped up ready to fight. I didn't have time for this. I had to get to Mahoney!

"Honey, it's me; it's Molly."

Oh, Molly. Okay, I didn't have to fight. Where did my keys go to? I needed my car keys.

"Do you see my keys, Molly? I need them to drive..."

Then I heard footsteps walking across the porch toward us. I looked over and saw Bert. An officer coming to the house after a shooting...

"Oh, no," I said backing away from them. I held my arm out straight in front of me. "Don't you dare come near me! Don't you dare tell me that Mahoney's..." I couldn't say it.

"She's in shock," Molly said to Bert.

"I see that."

"Honey, listen to me. Mahoney's okay. He's okay, do you understand?"

"Oh, Molly," I groaned. "Mahoney's been shot. Someone shot my Mahoney."

"Yes, honey, he's been shot." Molly moved close to me and put her arm on mine. "But he's okay."

"He's not..." That word. If I didn't say it, it had no power to be true.

"No. He's going to be fine."

"Then why...why are you here?"

"We came so you wouldn't be alone. We came to drive you to the hospital."

"But Molly, I can't lock the door. The key doesn't work."

Molly nodded at Bert who found the keys where they'd fallen. He picked them up and locked the door. Inside, Dorsey howled.

"See. Bert locked the door for you."

"Dorsey. I can't leave him howling like that. He's too upset."

Bert unlocked the door and opened it. Dorsey exploded from the house and ran to me. Mom, what's wrong? He looked at Molly and Bert. I know them; no danger there. I dropped down to the floor and buried my face in his fur. Dorsey whimpered. I know something's wrong, but I can't figure out what.

"Baby, I have to go out. I need you to be a good boy for me. Will you do that?"

Woof. "Sure, Mom." Woof, woof. "What do you want me to do?"

"I have a job for you." Dorsey sat up listening. "I want you to guard the house and take care of Charlie, okay?"

Woof. "Okay." Dorsey walked to the door, but stopped to look back at me before he entered. "Good boy," I said. He disappeared into the house, and Bert locked the door.

"Come on," Molly said as she helped me to get up. "Let's go see Mahoney."

When I saw Mahoney sitting up in bed smiling at me, I threw myself at him. At the last second, I saw the bandages on his arm and swiveled slightly to avoid hitting them. I draped my body across his and buried my face between his neck and shoulder away from the injured arm. The warmth of his body assured me.

"It's okay, Princess. I'm all right." He ran the hand on his good arm across my back then folded it across me in a hug. I'm not sure how long we stayed like that. Long enough for my heart to stop pounding.

"Hey, you're getting me wet."

I sat up beside him on the bed. I noticed then that we were alone. The others had left to give us privacy. Mahoney brushed the tears from my cheeks.

"Aren't you going to say anything?"

"I love you."

"I like your choice of words."

"Mahoney," I said, "don't you ever scare me like that again."

"Ah," he said, "feisty is good."

"Tell me what happened."

"I was on the way to my car, when this guy walked by

me. He looked at me...I'm not sure how to describe it. A little smug, a little like he was holding back a laugh. My antenna went up. I turned around to see where he was going just as he pulled the trigger. I jumped sideways, so the bullet only hit my arm."

"Only."

"Better than my back."

"True. Did you get a good look at him?"

"Absolutely. A police artist is on his way to make a sketch. I saw the guy when he passed me and again when I turned. As soon as he fired, he ran. I'm not sure if he even realizes he didn't kill me."

"He didn't look back?"

"No. We decided to put out the word that I was more seriously injured than I am, in case we can use it."

"Can you?"

"Still working on that. Bert said he'd come get you, and we figured he'd pick you up before you heard anything to the contrary." He put his hand across mine. "I'm really, really sorry, Princess, that it didn't work that way. When he called to tell me the state you were in, I was devastated."

"He called you? I don't remember his calling anyone."

"Apparently you were in shock. Do you remember what you did before Bert and Molly got you into the car?"

I searched my memory. "Not all of it. Only little snapshots."

He nodded. "Now we've got to figure out if I'm at death's door in the hospital..."

"Don't use that word."

"What word?"

"The 'd' word. I wouldn't let myself say it, and I don't want to hear it."

"Okay." He patted my hand. "Anyway, we're got to figure

out how I'm going to a wedding..."

"Oh my gosh, I forgot about the wedding."

"How could you forget about our wedding?"

"I was too worried about something else."

He raised my hand to his lips and kissed it.

"Do you want to cancel the wedding? I could call Mark and..."

"Woman, you are not canceling our wedding!" He said it loud enough that a nurse came running in to see if there was a problem.

I sat back against the pillow so we rested side by side.

"Okay, so we aren't canceling the wedding."

"But we still have to figure out how to get me there. We don't know who shot me or why. The lieutenant's afraid he might try again, especially since I know what he looks like. And not only me... We're got to keep everyone safe."

We sat quietly, thinking.

"I know. Let's do the 'pretend' thing again, only in reverse."

"Huh? Oh, you mean pretend to cancel the wedding... announce on the news that it's canceled, but have it for real, like in secret."

"Yup. But don't you guys dare announce the cancellation until after I've contacted everyone involved to let them know it's really not canceled." I touched him: his face, his arm, his chest. "Are you sure you're up to this? It won't be too much of a strain?"

"Marrying you is not a 'strain.' Besides, I'll have a whole week afterward to rest."

"Some honeymoon I'm going to have."

He leered at me. "I don't need that much rest."

"When can you come home?"

A doctor appeared in the doorway. "Maybe I can answer

that." As he came over to the bed, I got off it. "How do you feel?" he asked Mahoney.

"Fine."

"Pain?"

"Only a little."

"Let's take a look at the wound." The doctor started unwrapping the bandage. As he removed the protective gauze, I could see the blood-soaked layers underneath. I gasped.

The doctor stopped. "Perhaps you'd like to wait outside."

I would, but I couldn't. "I'm going to have to be changing that for him," I said. "I need to learn how to clean and dress it properly."

Mahoney grabbed my hand with his usable one and squeezed. Not for him, for me.

The doctor continued unwrapping. No need to describe how gruesome Mahoney's arm looked after the doctor completely removed the bandage.

"This is good," the doctor said. Good?

"The bleeding has stopped. That's a good sign."

A nurse came in to help the doctor clean the wound. Once they'd cleaned off the dry blood, the wound did look better.

"It's a flesh wound," the doctor told me. "Looks a whole lot worse than it really is."

"Does that mean he'll have full use of that arm?"

"No reason why he shouldn't. He'll have a scar, of course. Now pay attention while I redress it so you'll know what to do. First, put..."

I learned more about dressing a serious wound than I'd ever wanted to know. Hope I don't have to use that knowledge again.

Once the doctor finished, Mahoney asked, "So when can

I go home, Doc?"

"Tomorrow, for sure. We'd like to keep you under observation tonight."

"I'd *really* like to go home now."

The doctor studied Mahoney's chart. "I suppose you could." Mahoney squeezed my hand. "But if the wound starts bleeding again, I want you back here immediately." We promised. "And no heavy lifting or exertion with that arm. We'll put a sling on it to remind you. Keep it on until the wound closes. I'll sign the release papers at the nurse's desk and leave two prescriptions for you—an antibiotic and pain medication in case you need it." We thanked him and he left.

I helped Mahoney dress, and a nurse brought in a sling and adjusted it for him. Mahoney called the lieutenant and asked that the police artist be redirected to our house. Molly and Bert, who had stayed in the waiting room, joined us. They drove us home and went to the pharmacy for Mahoney's meds. On the way back, Molly dropped Bert off at the station, and he drove Mahoney's car home.

Chapter 22

With all the activity that went on that night, I almost wished Mahoney had stayed in the hospital and rested. Ernie, the police artist, came and made a sketch. The person in the sketch looked vaguely familiar to me. I asked Ernie to make another sketch and put sunglasses and a baseball cap on him. "That's him," I said. "That's the guy."

Lieutenant Palmer had come with Ernie. "What guy?" he asked.

I launched into an explanation of the driver who had stopped in front of the McGill house and stared at me. Between us, Mahoney and I connected the dots with other incidents. The vandalism of the McGill's car, the note left under the car windshield and its reference to my notes stolen before the show, the bracelet from an unknown sender. We included our theory that Bethany was behind the incidents, or at least connected to them. Bert and Mahoney explained their impressions during their interview with her. Of course, we had to mention the nagging discrepancies. A man and not a woman drove the car. The woman buying the bracelet did not fit Bethany's description. We ended with the transposed numbers of the street address.

"Sounds like she's not working alone," Palmer said. We agreed. "And if she's been after you," he looked at me, "the whole time, why shoot Mahoney?" Good question. "I don't like it. All we have is theories, no concrete evidence. You're both targets now and easy marks with your wedding on Saturday."

We shared our idea about a false notification to the news about having to cancel our wedding. He liked it. He'd take care of informing the press.

As soon as Palmer and Ernie left, I dug out my lists of wedding guests and those I'd hired for the event. It was late, so we had to postpone making the calls until the morning, except for Arlene and Arty and Eileen and Bill. They offered to help Molly, Bert, Mahoney, and me make the phone calls. Thank goodness for cell phones. With eight of us, we might meet Palmer's one o'clock deadline, when he planned to hold the press conference. No way would that happen with one house phone. Even with eight phones going at the same time, it wasn't the amount of calls we had to make that daunted us, but the time it took for each call. Everyone naturally wanted to hear the whole story and a report on how Mahoney was doing. We also swore them to secrecy.

I needed to go see Mark at the Cedar Inn. After Wednesday's fiasco, I'd told him not to believe any phone messages. I looked at the clock. I might make it out there before closing, and we had so much to do in the morning. Bert offered to drive me. He stuck his portable siren on the top of the car and whisked me away sirens blaring. It was kinda fun. The others kept Mahoney company until we returned.

When I saw Mahoney's eyelids droop, I kicked everyone out. I helped him undress, gave him his medication, and put him in bed. "I feel like a baby," he said.

"You are," I responded "my baby. I'm going to clean up the mess in the great room so we'll be ready for the morning, then I'll be back to join you." He was sound asleep when I returned.

We'd originally planned Friday as a relaxing day to take care of last minute necessities and set aside the clothes we planned to take on our honeymoon. It was anything but. My first item of business was to tend to Mahoney. Showering was awkward for him. Change the dressing on his wound. No new bleeding. Thank you, God. Dressing him, although he was getting better at fending for himself with one arm. Meds. I left him on the porch to enjoy his coffee and the view while I hopped into the shower.

I'd barely finished dressing when the gang arrived. Eileen and Arlene had both stopped for pastries, so we were well-stocked with snacks, and Molly brought sandwiches for lunch in case our phone calls took that long. They did. But we finished before our 1:00 deadline. Mahoney turned on the TV, and we all sat down to watch Palmer's press conference.

As expected, Palmer started by referencing Mahoney's shooting. "As you know, yesterday at approximately 5:00, Detective Jack Mahoney..." etc. etc. "Detective Mahoney sustained very serious injuries to his torso and has been moved to a private facility for care and treatment. Because of these injuries, his wedding which was scheduled for tomorrow, had to be canceled. We hope that anyone with information about the shooting or about the person responsible will call our tip line."

The expected questions and answers:

"Will he survive?"—"We certainly hope so."

"What facility has he been moved to?"—"I won't answer that."

"Will he reschedule the wedding?"—"We hope he will be able to do so."

Reporters shouted out questions about the investigation, which of course, he said he couldn't comment on. Why do they insist on asking questions they know won't be answered? I especially hate their stupid "How do you feel about..." questions. "How do you feel about one of your officers being shot and almost dying?" "How do you feel about your fiancé being shot and having to cancel your wedding?" Duh.

"Well, at least we know what private facility he's been moved to," Bill said. We all laughed.

"Why didn't you stay in the same hospital? Why pretend to move you?"

"Too many people involved. Too much potential leakage. We're taking a chance with the number of people who know the wedding really isn't canceled, but hoping since most of them are friends, they'll keep quiet."

After the gang left, I told Mahoney to take a nap. He didn't want to, said he felt fine. I said that if he didn't at least go lie down for awhile, when I went to have my hair styled in the morning, I'd have them cut it all off. He likes my hair; he went to the bedroom. I checked ten minutes later, and he was asleep. Good. He'd lost a lot of blood, and his body needed to replenish itself as well as tend to his wound. Sleep heals.

I looked at the clock. We were supposed to have had a rehearsal in an hour. I'd already told Mark we wouldn't be there, and told Bert the same thing in the car. He'd tell Molly. I didn't mention it to Mahoney. He'd probably forgotten about it, and his sleep was far more important.

I took Dorsey for a walk to get rid of my nervous energy and keep the house quiet. As we approached the McGill house, Jim came out to pick up his mail, and I stopped to say hello. He pulled the mail from his box. On top of the regular mail lay a thick folded sheet of paper.

"I wonder what this is," he said and opened it.

"My God!"

He handed the paper to me which turned out to be a copy of the poster from our Blakely event. Across my photo, someone wrote, "You got what you deserved."

I took my cell out of my pocket and called Bert. I had no intention of upsetting Mahoney with this. Bert told me to stay where I was and he'd come pick it up.

It was awkward standing there with Jim while I waited. I didn't know if he'd connected this event to the others at his house. "Why would they leave it in my mailbox?" he asked.

Okay, so he hadn't—yet. I knew the no-no rule about giving out information during an on-going investigation. Sure, Mahoney and I ignored the rule, but that was different than sharing the information with Jim. I felt bad about his innocent involvement and the damages he'd incurred to his house and car, mostly his car, but all I could do at the moment was pretend I didn't know.

Alice appeared in the front doorway. "Jim, what's taking you so long?" Then she saw me. "Oh, hi!" She walked across the lawn to join us. Hurry up, Bert, hurry.

"We got another one of those strange notes." I'd dropped the poster when I called Bert. He bent down to pick it up.

"Jim, don't." He stopped midway. "Why?"

"Fingerprints."

"But I've already touched it."

"Yes, and you could smear other prints if you touch it again."

"Oh." He straightened back up.

Alice stood by us now and looked down at the poster. It had landed face up, and my picture stared up at us. "How horrible!"

Bert to the rescue. He pulled up alongside us. He used tongs to put the poster into a plastic bag. "Did you touch it?" he asked Jim.

"Yes, when I took the mail out of the box and opened it."

"We're going to need your prints for elimination purposes."

"Anything I can do to help." He paused for a moment. "Does this have anything to do with the vandalism of our car?" So he was connecting the dots.

"At this point, I can't say. We'll need to analyze it for prints first." The great non-committal response.

"I'm so sorry." I said to Jim and Alice.

"There's nothing for you to be sorry about," Jim responded. "You didn't do this."

"How horrible for you to have to go through this!" Alice added.

Bert packed Dorsey and me into the car just to get us out of an awkward situation.

"Doesn't she ever give up?" I asked Bert. He knew who I meant.

"That's what worries me. Who knows what she'll do next. The good part of this is that if she did this, she's now committed a federal crime."

"Tampering with the mail?"

Bert nodded. "And if her prints are on it, we finally have some tangible evidence of harassment. Are you okay?"

"I'm just sick of her. All I want to think about right now is Mahoney getting better, our wedding, and our honeymoon."

Bert leaned over and kissed my cheek. "You do exactly that. Leave this to us."

Chapter 23

Mahoney had a bad night. He kept rolling over on his side—the one with his bad arm. He'd yelp and wake up which woke me up. I was ready to tie him down on his back. Not very sympathetic of me.

When the alarm sounded in the morning, I groggily reached over to turn it off. Mahoney wasn't working today. He must have set it by mistake. Oops, no, it's our wedding day! The alarm was for me. I had an early morning appointment with a hair stylist.

I rarely go to a beauty parlor except to have my hair cut. My curls have a mind of their own and defy anyone's attempt to force them into submission. But I so wanted to dress up my hair for my wedding. What girl doesn't? And I'd never be doing this again. As Jennie DeLane had said when Mahoney and I first dated with our future a bumpy road because of my living hundreds of miles away, "A house can be replaced. A Mahoney can't." She was so right. Today was a one shot deal.

I'd found a beauty parlor in the yellow pages named Tangles. A perfect description of my hair. I'd made an appointment for a dry run, and the stylist did a good job pinning my hair up with cascades of curls falling down. I hoped she'd recreate that this morning.

When I got to Tangles, the stylist Julie looked up in

surprise. "But you canceled your appointment."

Oh, oh, not again. "No," I said. "I didn't."

"I did think it odd because you couldn't remember the time of your appointment and said something about a cut instead of just a styling...but I've already booked someone else."

She peeked at her appointment book as another customer joined us.

"I could fit you in at 11:30."

"That won't work. My wedding's at 12:00."

"I'm sorry..."

The other customer interrupted her.

"I couldn't help but overhear part of your conversation. Today's your wedding?"

"And someone canceled her appointment. Can you believe that? I gave it to you."

"And you said you had an opening at 11:30?"

"Yes."

"Put me down for 11:30; I'll come back."

I wanted to kiss her but restrained myself.

"Oh, thank you so much!"

"You're very welcome. It's more important that you have your hair done...and have a blessed day."

While Julie changed her appointment book, I mentally scanned my 'to do' list. What else might this 'someone' have changed? We ordered the wedding cake through Mark; that was safe. The florist...the florist?

I quickly picked up my phone and punched in their number. Yes, my flower order had been canceled too. Fortunately, we hadn't ordered too many flowers. The girls and I had made centerpieces for the tables, and Eileen said she'd delivered those yesterday. From the florist, I'd ordered baby breath for my hair in lieu of a veil, boutonnieres for

Mahoney and Bert—his best man—a corsage for Molly—my matron of honor—and a bouquet for me to carry. No exotic or special order types of flowers. Yes, they could still put the order together and have it ready on time.

Julie waited for me to finish the conversation.

"They canceled your flower order too?" I nodded. "Wow! Who would do something like that?"

Who indeed? I wanted to wring that reporter's neck for putting the announcement of our wedding in the newspaper almost as much as I wanted to wring Bethany's! He'd included the name of the Cedar Inn, so I understood the call to Mark. But the stylist and florist? 'Someone' spent a lot of time phoning beauty parlors and florists.

When we returned from our honeymoon, I wanted an end to this harassment. Our honeymoon? I'd check with the hotel as soon as my hair was done. What else could go wrong today? At least I'd fed the beauty parlor with plenty to gossip about for days to come.

Chapter 24

I waited in a small room for the music to start. Molly and Dorsey waited with me. I wasn't really into the walk down the aisle business, but Mahoney wanted me to. He said he wanted the time to appreciate how beautiful I looked without any interruptions. Mark had set an arch in the garden surrounded by colorful plants. My Prince waited for me under it.

We didn't have a flower girl or ring bearer. We let Dorsey play that role. I'd made a special pouch to attach to his harness for him to carry the rings. No leash. I hoped he wouldn't stop along the way to visit with the guests he knew, or we might have a comic wedding instead of a romantic one.

The music started. Molly walked in front as my matron of honor. Dorsey should have followed her, but he walked by my side. That was okay with me. I'd canceled the rehearsal to save Mahoney's energy. The minister would position Mahoney and Bert; I'd shown Molly where to stand from a window in the reception room. The only member of the wedding party who really needed a rehearsal was Dorsey. Oh, well. I told him to stay by my side, and he was doing just that.

I saw a blur of faces on either side of me and noticed blue uniforms around the perimeter. So some guys like to stand rather than sit. All I saw clearly was that handsome man waiting for me under the arbor. A year ago I'd vowed never to get involved with a man again, and here I was walking toward the man I loved to become his wife.

When we reached the end of the aisle, Mahoney took my hand. We waited while Bert removed the rings from the pouch. Dorsey then lay down and quietly watched the two of us during the entire ceremony.

Mahoney and I turned toward the minister and it began. It doesn't take long to exchange those promises of love and fidelity, but a lifetime to live them. Oh, happy lifetime! When we exchanged rings, I took care in slipping Mahoney's on his finger because I didn't want to bump his injured arm. Then the minister said, "I now pronounce you man and wife." Oh, wonderful words! As Mahoney kissed me, our guests burst out clapping and cheering. Dorsey jumped up and joined them, barking and running rings around us. I'd give the photographer an extra tip if he'd caught that on video.

During the reception while we were visiting with guests, I lost track of Mahoney. Concerned because of his injury, I excused myself to go find him. Someone pointed toward the front door. I opened it as Mahoney thanked a uniform and slipped a piece of paper into his pocket. The officer walked toward the perimeter of the parking lot. Only then did I notice other officers stationed around the perimeter. My memory jumped back to the time I walked down the aisle. I'd seen uniforms stationed around the perimeter then too.

"Mahoney?"

He spun around. "Hi, honey."

"What's going on?" I gestured toward the officers.

He shrugged. "A little protection, just in case. Think of them as our honor guard."

"Palmer must have spent a fortune in overtime."

"Didn't cost him a cent."

Mahoney put his good arm around my shoulder. "Let's go back in."

"Wait. What do you mean it didn't cost him a cent?"

"They're all volunteers."

"These guys all volunteered to do this?"

"They did. Every guy on the force thinks the world of you after what you did for Blakely. And after my being shot... Palmer asked for volunteers to guard us today and there they are."

"And they've been out here this whole time?"

"Yes."

When we went inside, I asked a waiter to find Mark for me. He came immediately.

"Is everything okay? Is there a problem?"

"Mark, this day has been perfect. You and your staff did a superb job." He beamed. "I just have a request."

"Anything."

"Could you get a waiter to make up plates from the food on the buffet table and bring them to the officers outside? And maybe some water or soda or something?"

"Certainly." Mark hailed a passing waiter and stepped aside to give him instructions.

Mahoney kissed my cheek. "And that, Princess, is why they like you so much."

We returned to the reception and stayed a while longer, but I noticed Mahoney's movements slowing. He was getting tired. I leaned over and whispered in his ear, "I think it's time to take our leave."

"But it's such a good party."

"It is. But you have some husbandly duties to perform this evening, and I don't want to hear any excuses about being too tired."

111

"In that case, let's go."

Neither of us had driven. Mahoney couldn't, and the bride doesn't. We signaled to our chauffer Bert who drove us, and Dorsey, home.

I have a habit when I hang up clothes or throw them into the laundry basket to check pockets. I hate when paper or especially tissues end up in the washing machine. So as I hung up Mahoney's jacket, I reached into the pocket and found a piece of paper. On it were written the make and model of a black car and the license plate number. I pictured him slipping it into his pocket when he'd been talking to the officer outside the restaurant.

"Mahoney, what's this?"

Mahoney was in the bathroom trying a one-armed version of shaving.

"This paper in your pocket." I showed it to him.

"Oh, that, umm."

"Don't." I knew he was dreaming up a phony story.

He grinned a 'we know each other pretty well, don't we' grin.

"A car pulled into the parking lot at the restaurant. The driver looked surprised and drove back out. That's all that happened, but Palmer told the guys to note down anything unusual, even the littlest thing."

"Did he say who was in the car?"

"A couple."

"That's it? No description?"

"The woman had blonde hair." Why didn't that surprise me? "And?"

"That's it. Really. Now don't let your imagination blow this out of proportion. It could easily have been a couple coming for dinner, and it surprised them to see the parking lot so full and cops standing around so they just turned around and left."

"So coincidences are okay today?" He doesn't believe in coincidences.

"No, but it's not my worry right now. Bert will look into it. My concern right now is how to get this shaving cream off my face. It's a little hard wringing out a face cloth with one hand."

I laughed and helped him, and we climbed into our marital bed. Honestly, it didn't feel any different than it had the night before, which was a good thing. We joke and tease about sex, but our joining expresses our deepest love for each other and has since the day he first carried me into his bedroom. The bed was, is, and will remain our special place of "us-ness."

Chapter 25

We'd planned to leave on our honeymoon by 10:00 Sunday morning. I looked at the clock. 11:45. And we were nowhere near ready. Friday's chores on our going away 'to do' list remained untouched, plus we had Sunday morning's tasks. Pick the clothes to take and pack the suitcases, take Dorsey and Charlie and all their stuff—also not yet packed—over to Jennie's, tidy up the house. Oh, yes, and get ourselves ready. Not such an easy task for my one-armed man. Most of the chores, too, required two arms. Ever try to fold clothes and put them in a suitcase with one hand? So while I rushed about, Mahoney fumed from frustration at not being able to help. He threatened to take the sling off and use the arm. I told him if he did, I'd be applying for a divorce on Monday.

I picked up the phone to call Jennie for the third time that morning to change the time for dropping the kids off. Wait. Here's a job Mahoney can do. So instead of dialing, I walked the phone over to Mahoney who sat at the kitchen island drumming his fingers on the countertop. I handed the phone to him.

"Will you call Jennie and tell her another half hour or so?"

"Sure." I think he was relieved to have something he could do.

I heard them chatting as I packed cat food and dog food and toys and treats and their dishes and leashes and did I forget anything? I set up Charlie's cat carrier. Charlie immediately disappears when the carrier appears, so I assigned Dorsey the job of finding her.

"You're sure? It's not a problem?" Mahoney asked.

I couldn't hear the reply.

"Yeah, it would help a lot. Thanks. 20 minutes? Okay."

Mahoney smiled. "One less thing we need to do. Jennie's coming over to pick them up."

"That'll help a lot. I think I've got their stuff ready to go. Want to help me take it out to the porch so we can just throw it in the truck when she gets here?" He could easily handle picking stuff up with one hand and carrying it.

"Why don't I do that while you finish packing?"

"Deal. Don't take out the cat carrier yet."

I went back to the bedroom to fold the last of my 'to go' pile into the suitcase. Woof, woof. Dorsey had found Charlie. He came running into the room to lead me to her. "Good boy," I said and followed him into the laundry room. He squeezed his nose between the washer and dryer. I looked behind the dryer. Sure enough, there she was. Now how did she get in there and how was I going to get her out?

"Honey, where are you?"

"Laundry room."

The man himself appeared in the doorway. "What's up?"

"Charlie hid behind the dryer. How the heck are we going to get her out?"

Fortunately, dryers are comparatively light. We slid it out far enough to give Charlie an escape route without having to disconnect the electrical cord and exhaust duct, but it wasn't far enough for either one of us to reach back and get her. The hectic morning was catching up to me.

"I'm tempted to leave her there."

"How about you get the vacuum cleaner out of the closet instead?"

"The vacuum clean...Mahoney, you're brilliant!"

Charlie absolutely hates the vacuum cleaner. She'll run as far away from the noise as possible.

Mahoney turned the machine on, and Charlie jumped out of her hidey-hole. I managed to grab hold of her. Harnesses are handy for more than attaching a leash. She squirmed and pushed, but I held on long enough to get her into the carrier. She mewed at the unfairness of it.

As I finished zipping up the side of the carrier, Jennie pulled into the driveway. Dorsey immediately ran to the door barking. "Someone's here, someone's here!" Mahoney picked up the carrier, I opened the door, and Dorsey darted outside. One of Jennie's dogs jumped down from the rear of the truck. Oh, happy days! Dorsey was friends with Jennie's dogs. The two of them sniffed hello and took off for a romp around the yard.

"I figured if I brought Hercules with me, he'd distract Dorsey when we leave."

He did. We loaded the kids and their stuff into the truck and thanked Jennie. Charlie cried, mostly because she hates cages and cars, but Dorsey was too excited about being with Hercules and going for a ride in the truck to notice us wave goodbye.

"What's left to do, Princess?"

"Close the suitcases. You put them in the car while I freshen up and we're off. Oh, and would you call the inn to tell them we'll be arriving late?"

Twenty minutes later we drove off to five days of "us-ness." No schedules, no chores, no bad guys, no Bethany. Halleluiah!

Chapter 26

For our honeymoon, Mahoney and I had booked reservations in a small lakeside lodge in the mountains. No one had messed with that, mostly because no one knew where we were headed except Mahoney and me and the hotel.

Our room on the top floor offered complete privacy. Nobody but the birds could see in through the window, or more precisely, the French doors that opened onto a balcony overlooking the lake. We enjoyed seeing the lake by day and the stars by night. From the balcony, we watched sunsets and sunrises and the mid-day sun coating the surface of the water with little diamonds.

Some plans changed. We'd originally wanted to learn kayaking and set up some lessons. We'd arranged with a stable to take a group horseback trek up the mountainside. All canceled. Even if Mahoney could manage, his arm was too weak. Who cares? I'd almost lost him. Having him by my side was all that mattered.

We contented ourselves with walks along the lakeside paths or hikes through the woods or exploring the nearby towns. We bought a couple of old-fashioned outdoor lanterns for the new patio and a soft hand knit green throw for a reading chair in the office. I said 'no' to a wood carving of a bear smoking a pipe, but okay to a hand carved squirrel munching on a nut. He's really cute! We slept-in or woke up early, we ate when we wanted, and of course, we fulfilled our obligations as honeymooners. We did lots of that.

On Tuesday morning, Mahoney threw away his sling. The gunshot wound had closed. I dug out a bottle of vitamin E oil I'd stashed away in the suitcase and prepared to apply it to his skin. He didn't want me to. I explained that if he applied it every day, the vitamin E helps heal the skin and could lessen the scarring. He still didn't want me to. I asked him, "Please, please, do it for me." He let me apply it. I restrained from saying "I told you so" when Mahoney went to the doctor for a checkup a month later. The doctor marveled at the small amount of scarring compared to what he had expected. Mahoney winked at me.

All too soon we packed up our bags again for the four-hour drive home. By mutual consent, we avoided any mention of bank robberies, shootings, and Bethany during the honeymoon. But as the miles brought us closer to Cedar Falls, Mahoney itched to know what progress had been made on the cases since our departure. He was officially off-duty until a doctor and the department cleared him to return to work, but yearned to go in for a few hours to catch up. I agreed he should. I didn't want our safety to be a high-stakes game any longer.

I told him then about the poster in the McGill's mailbox and how 'someone' had canceled my hair appointment and the florist order. I expected him to be upset; he was. But after reminding him of his physical condition at the time, and how he couldn't do anything about it, he understood why I'd kept silent. He wanted to know if I'd told anyone, and I said 'no,' but since the stylist knew about the cancellations, the whole town was probably aware by now once the beauty parlor gossip spread. He laughed at the idea until he found out it was true.

We stopped at the DeLane's to pick up Dorsey and Charlie. Charlie appeared her normal nonchalant self until we got home. After letting her out of the carrier, she stayed by my side wherever I went. I left my unpacked suitcase open that night on a chair. She jumped up and curled inside it to sleep. You're not going again without me!

Dorsey, on the other hand, was barking and dancing on his hind legs when we pulled up. When Mahoney opened his door, Dorsey wanted to climb in his lap. Mahoney allowed only two paws up. Once they exchanged greetings, Dorsey tried to jump over Mahoney to get to me. I opened my car door and told him to come around the car. Such joy! Animals can make you feel so loved. Greetings over, he stood in front of the back door and woofed. "Let me in."

Pete and Jennie DeLane came out to greet us with some of the kids' stuff in hand. I chatted with them while Mahoney brought the rest down from their porch. Dorsey's woofs turned into impatient barks. He tried separating me from the group and herding me toward the car. "Come on, Mom, I've got to get home."

We laughed at his antics and said our goodbyes. Dorsey told us all the way home what a great vacation he'd enjoyed. Charlie howled. I guess she didn't agree with him.

Chapter 27

The other Cedar Falls detectives had been quite busy during Mahoney's absence. The lab lifted Bethany's fingerprints from the poster left in the McGill's mailbox and from the note left under the McGill's windshield wipers. How did they know the prints were Bethany's? Her former boss at the car dealership allowed the CSI's to take prints from her office there for comparison.

That concrete evidence plus all the circumstantial evidence was enough to issue a warrant for her arrest for harassment, and the FBI might add a federal warrant for tampering with the mail.

The lab also lifted another set of unknown prints from both the poster and the note. The unknown prints from both belonged to the same person. That confirmed an accomplice.

The car that pulled into the Cedar Inn's parking lot and quickly exited on the day of our wedding belonged to an Eric Handley. That in itself was nothing, but the photo on Handley's driver's license matched the sketch the artist had drawn the night Mahoney was shot. Nailed.

Now to connect Handley as Bethany's accomplice. Mahoney had left his notes on the case with Bert. Bert thumbed through them and found the full name, address, and phone number of the only person who had written a letter to the editor in Bethany's defense after she attacked me in the newspaper—E. Handley. That address matched Handley's address on his license. Not conclusive, but telling. When the police arrested him for the attempted murder of Mahoney, they'd fingerprint him. No one doubted those prints would match the unknown prints from the poster and the note left on the McGill's car.

Mahoney showed up at the department on Friday right after all the *i*'s had been dotted and the *t*'s crossed on the arrest warrants. Two sets of detectives stood by: one pair to arrest Bethany, the other pair to go after Handley. Mahoney wanted to join them, but the lieutenant couldn't let him since he was still officially off-duty.

Palmer told Mahoney to go get a doctor to sign a release, while he prepared and signed the department's release. It would take a little time for the arrests to be made and the suspects brought back to the station. Palmer told him they'd let the suspects fret in the interrogation rooms if necessary until Mahoney returned.

Mahoney phoned me to tell me what was happening. I could hear the lilt in his voice. I was quietly dancing around the room while I listened to him.

"I want to be there, Mahoney."

"Ah, Princess, I don't have the authority to okay that. I promise to tell you everything tonight."

Mahoney didn't have the authority, but Palmer did. I called the lieutenant. I knew I'd never be allowed in the interrogation room, but hoped I could stand behind the two-way mirror. Did they have those kinds of room? Naturally, his first response was negative.

I can be pretty good at begging if I have to—or be a real pain, depending on how you look at it. I gave him a zillion reasons why he should let me. I was the only one present during some of the harassment and could catch her lies. I was the only one who knew the details of their trying to sabotage our wedding. I...I...I. Finally I threw my zinger at him. Hadn't I helped them with this and that?

He relented. I think he just wanted to stop me from badgering him. He wouldn't let me near the interrogation rooms, but I could stay in the AV room where they taped the interviews. Good enough.

Three hours later the detectives entered the interrogation rooms—one room for Bethany and a different one for Eric Handley. Mahoney, Palmer, and I stayed in the AV room where we watched both interviews at the same time. Better than a two-way mirror into one room!

Palmer wanted Mahoney to listen to the other detectives lay the foundation, then surprise Eric and Bethany with Mahoney's appearance. They might not know he's all right. Suspicious, yes. They'd seen the full parking lot at the Cedar Inn on our wedding day and the cops standing around the perimeter. But no one had seen either one of us for days. Mahoney's reporter friend had kept the question of Mahoney's health alive with short articles in the newspaper.

Eric sat back in his chair with his arms folded over his chest and a smirk on his face. The tough guy. He didn't know what they were talking about. The sketch of him was either a plant or a coincidence. He didn't know any Bethany.

Then why had he written a letter to the editor in her defense?

He had a right to his opinion, didn't he?

Meanwhile the lab was processing the fingerprints they'd taken when they brought Eric to the station and running a comparison with those from the poster and the note on the McGill's car.

In the other interrogation room, Bethany examined her nails or smoothed wrinkles in her clothes. When Bert and

Arty started questioning her, her hair became the favored target of her fidgeting. She toyed with it until strands worked their way out of her coiffure and hung limply around her face.

At first, she too denied knowing anything about the incidents or Eric. When presented with the poster and the note with evidence of both their fingerprints on it, it became "Oh, that Eric." She didn't know his last name was Handley. She only hung around with him when she had nothing better to do. Besides, it was only a prank.

On cue, the FBI agent entered the room. No, it was a violation of federal law.

Bethany looked from one to the other. "You're kidding, right? All we did was put something in the mailbox."

"Under federal law, the U.S. Postal Service has exclusive use of a mailbox."

Bethany's "Huh?" prompted him to continue. "Meaning only the USPS may place mail or any other item in a mailbox. The USPS also requires that any item placed in a mailbox must have the required amount of postage. So you broke the law on two accounts."

"But that's..."

"The penalty for tampering with the mail is five years in prison and/or a fine."

"Five years in..." Bethany's shoulders sagged.

Bert and Arty moved on to the McGill's car. No. no. They had it all wrong. She only put the note under the windshield wipers. Eric did the rest. It was just another prank.

No, Arty informed her, it was vandalism. He didn't add then that conspiracy in the commission of a crime made her just as responsible for the vandalism as Eric.

And why had they vandalized the McGill's car? She didn't know any McGill. They'd vandalized my car. When

Bert told her they'd mixed up the address, she sank lower into her chair. "It wasn't hers?" she mumbled to the table.

Bethany's list of offenses was growing. But the most important was yet to come. First, however, they asked her about sending me the bracelet.

She looked totally bewildered. What bracelet? She didn't know anything about a bracelet. I believed her. Bert and Arty had broken her down too far for such complete, forthright denial.

But, then, who sent me the bracelet? And why? Had the girls been right? A fan? No, that didn't account for the address mix-up. I agreed with Mahoney on this one. It was no coincidence.

Now the biggie. Why had Eric shot Mahoney? She put her head down on the table and sobbed.

"Okay, Mahoney, you're on," Palmer said.

At this point, I think Mahoney had forgotten I was in the room. He focused only on that interrogation room. When he opened the door to the room, he nodded to Bert, Arty, and the FBI agent who gathered up their papers and left. Mahoney leaned against the door with his arms folded across his chest. He waited patiently.

When Bethany's tears subsided, she looked up and realized Bert and Arty no longer sat across from her at the table and gazed around the room. She spotted Mahoney and jerked upright.

"You're alive? You're okay?"

"I am."

"Thank God!" She pushed her hair back from her face and patted it down. Sorry, Bethany, it's going to take a lot more than that to fix it.

"I'm so sorry you were hurt. I didn't want that."

Mahoney walked over to the table.

"If you didn't want to see me hurt, why did you try to kill me?"

"Oh, Jack, I would never do that. It was Eric."

"Why did Eric want to kill me?"

"Eric likes me. That's how I got him to help me to scare... *her*." The hateful emphasis on 'her' left no doubt who 'her' was.

"I wanted to get rid of her so we could be together." Mahoney flinched. "Then he told me he was tired of playing games and that he was going after you so I'd stop thinking about you."

"You knew ahead of time and didn't bother to warn me or anyone else in the department?"

The guys in the AV room cheered. Under the conspiracy in the furtherance of crime statutes, she had just earned herself a charge of attempted murder of a police officer.

"But I broke up with him. I told him I didn't want to see him anymore. I thought that would stop him, so we..."

"And after he did shoot me, why didn't you come forward?"

She reached her arm out toward him.

"I'm sorry, Jack. I was just so confused. All I wanted was the day when you and I..."

Mahoney walked back to the door and opened it. Before he left, he turned back to her.

"You are confused. There is no 'we' or 'you and I.' There never was and there never will be."

The detectives had left Eric by himself in the other interrogation room. He had leaned his chair back on two legs and put his feet up on the table and his hands behind his head. When Mahoney walked in, Eric pulled his feet off the table and the chair fell on all four legs.

"Yeah," Mahoney said, "You missed me."

"I didn't miss you. I hit you. I saw you spin from the impact before..." Eric stopped himself. He'd just confessed. Another cheer rose from the AV room.

"Your girlfriend had a lot to say about you."

"That stupid b... what girlfriend?"

So he was dummying up again. He wasn't going to incriminate himself the way Bethany had, but it didn't matter too much. He'd said enough.

"I want a lawyer." Interrogation over.

Chapter 28

The guys wanted to go to the local dive to celebrate. I told Mahoney to go with them. Mahoney spent his time either working or being with me. I, on the other hand, spent some leisure time with the girls having lunch or shopping. He needed some 'guy' time.

Once home, I went to visit my office. It still needed insulation, dry walling, molding, flooring, and painting. I turned on the overhead lights, not because I needed to, but because I could. The contractor had completed all the electrical work during our absence. Diffused light still shone through the closed shades. We opted to buy the French doors and windows with the blinds built in, embedded between two panes of glass. Yeah! No cleaning blinds.

Since my insurance check from the bombing and subsequent fire had arrived, I insisted on paying for the upgrades to Mahoney's original plans. He didn't want me to. I told him it would help me feel more like this was 'our' house. He let me.

For me, the office was a symbol of our future. We'd planned the final version of it together and would choose the furnishings for it together.

I did by now feel a bit sorry for Bethany. I understood the magnetic attraction to Mahoney; I felt it myself. What got her into trouble was her refusal to accept that her attraction to him wasn't reciprocated. All I'd really wanted was for her to stop interfering with me and go away. Guess in a way we were similar there too. She wanted to get rid of me. Unfortunately for her, her methods of trying to make me 'go away' broke a few too many laws.

Love. She loved Mahoney, Eric loved her, and Mahoney loved me. I became the fourth person in the triangle. Triangles don't come in fours.

I wandered over to the outside doors and opened them. No patio yet. Mahoney had planned to pour a cement slab or use the pavers one finds in all the box stores. I wanted flagstone. Not only did I like the look of it, but I liked that we could contour the edges of the patio into graceful curves. Another upgrade.

He liked the flagstone too. The problem arose over who would lay it. I wanted to hire a mason; he wanted to do it himself. I never questioned his ability; I just wanted it done quickly. I could think of better ways for him to spend his free time—like us spending time together.

Mahoney came home a couple of hours later. He wasn't much of a drinker; neither one of us was. It had been his first full day of normal police activity, and I'm happy to say he didn't seem overly tired, although I noticed him favoring his arm a bit. He opened the refrigerator.

"Not much here." We hadn't been food shopping since our return. He opened the freezer.

"Why don't we go out?" I suggested. "We'll go shopping tomorrow."

He closed the freezer. "Any particular place in mind?"

"No."

"Let's go to the Cedar Inn. I like their food." From Mahoney, that was an A+ recommendation.

Mark greeted us like old friends and marveled at the

improvement in Mahoney. Several tables were open, and like most cops, Mahoney preferred to be seated where his back would be to the wall. They don't like the idea of anyone sneaking up on them. Mark gladly let Mahoney pick the table.

Mahoney couldn't completely let go of the successful day in arresting Bethany and Eric and our conversation drifted into cop talk.

"We still have to find the gun. Prosecutors love having the weapon; it makes their job so much easier. We'll search his place tomorrow morning."

"You're not worried about someone coming in overnight and taking it and hiding it for him?"

"We've kept the arrest under wrap so the news isn't out yet, and he isn't allowed phone privileges. We sealed off his apartment and have a uniform on the door. Should be fine till morning."

They ripped apart Eric's apartment the next morning, but couldn't find the gun. They stood in the living room.

"Damn," said Mahoney.

"Any place we could have missed?" Bert asked.

The uniform stationed at the door came in. "There's this neighbor keeps coming over and asking questions about Handley. Would one of you talk to her?"

Mahoney followed him to the door.

Mrs. Kincaid, who Mahoney later described as rather mousy looking, asked, "Is Eric all right? Has something happened to him?"

Mahoney 'answered' by asking questions of his own. How long had she known Eric? Were they close?

"I don't really know him very well," she said. "We're just friendly in a neighborly sort of way. Sometimes I do a favor for him, or he helps me out, that sort of thing. But he gave me a package to keep for him, and if something's happened to him, I don't want to be responsible for it."

Mahoney's instincts bristled. What kind of package? What was in it? She didn't know.

"It's all taped up," she explained. "I didn't open it."

Mahoney called Bert, and the two of them followed Mrs. Kincaid into her apartment. She reached into a closet and handed them a shoe-sized box.

"Thank you, mam, we'll take care of this for you."

"But Eric," she persisted, "is he all right?"

"He's under arrest," Bert said.

"Under arrest? Eric? For what?"

"For attempted murder."

The woman raised her hands to her mouth as she gasped. "Eric?"

"Are you okay, mam?" Bert asked.

"Yes, yes. It's just such a shock."

Mahoney and Bert thanked her for her help and returned to Eric's apartment. Their fingers itched to open the box. Inside, as they hoped, they found a gun. They gave each other a 'high-five' and reclosed the box.

One of the uniforms asked if they wanted him to bring it to the ballistics lab. Neither one of them wanted to take any chance of something going wrong. They took it to the lab themselves.

Mahoney and I were restocking our refrigerator after our much needed trip to the market.

"I can't wait to get the results from ballistics. I'm sure they'll match the slug from my arm."

I stopped and stared at the oranges I held in my hand.

"Something wrong with those?" Mahoney took one of the oranges.

"No, they're fine." I looked up at him. "Did you say the

woman was mousy looking?"

"Yah." He put the orange into the frig.

"And they did favors for each other?"

"Yah, so?" He took the other oranges from me and placed them in the bin.

"And the clerk couldn't remember anything distinctive about the woman who bought that bracelet for me? Someone too mousy looking to remember?"

"The one piece in all this that didn't fit." He gave me a kiss. "Want to go for a ride?"

"After we finish putting these groceries away."

Mrs. Kincaid recognized Mahoney and let us in.

Yes, she had gone to the Beads 'n Things to buy a present for Eric to give to a friend and have it mailed. He thought she might be better at picking out a woman's gift.

Why the Beads 'n Things? That was her choice; Eric didn't care what she bought or where she bought it. She liked the shop because they sold one-of-a-kind pieces. So much nicer for a gift.

Did she know why he wanted to send the gift? It was a thank you for something the woman had done for him. She wasn't sure exactly what. He had said she'd brought him closer to the woman he loved. So romantic, wasn't it?

So romantic, right. Bethany had turned to him to help her go after me.

She hadn't done anything wrong, had she? No, I assured her; it's comforting to know we can count on neighbors to help us. That appeased her. Did we know if the woman liked the gift? Yes, I assured her again; she liked it very much. I complimented Mrs. Kincaid on her good taste. The woman smiled happily. So did Mahoney. That tied up the loose ends.

On the way home, we stopped at a furniture store.

Neither one of us liked the style of their office furniture, nor was Mahoney too happy with the construction of it. I did see a reading chair that had possibilities. We also stopped at a sporting goods store where Mahoney purchased a hand ball squeezer to exercise his arm.

"It's gotten weak," he said, "just in that short period of time I couldn't use it."

The ball became his constant companion. He likes his body buff. Me too.

Chapter 29

Mahoney and I sat on our usual perches on the front porch. He threw a ball into the yard for Dorsey to chase, and I cuddled Charlie in my lap.

"So," I said, "that takes care of one shooting. What's happening with Blakely's?"

"Wong is still our favorite suspect, at least as far as being in on the robbery, but we've dug as far as we can. According to the neighbors, he had some Asian or Asian American visitors during the time the robbery took place, but we can't identify who or exactly when they were here. Again, the school won't cooperate in any way. Some of the guys think they're in on it."

"Absolutely not," I said. "Mrs. Higgins is dedicated to that school. She'd never do anything to jeopardize it."

"Isn't that the motive Wong supposedly has, to help the school?"

"Wanting to help the school is not the same as wanting to protect it. Besides, if she had been in on it in some way, why point out the new construction to me and talk about where the money to fund it came from? She was quite open about it. Wouldn't she have tried to hide what they were doing?"

Dorsey came running up and dropped his ball at Mahoney's feet. When Mahoney didn't respond, Dorsey put his foot on the ball and woofed. "More, Dad." Mahoney mechanically picked it up and threw it.

"I wish I could talk to her. She's not helping the school or herself with her silence. Did you read the latest 'update' in the paper? Another reporter practically accused her in particular of being part of the scheme."

I continued to pet Charlie but focused in the distance.

"This relationship you have with 'your' reporter? He does you a favor, then you owe him one, or the other way around, right?"

"We don't keep a running tally, but, yes, that's the way it works."

"And he hasn't been able to get any information from the Sign Language Center or interviews with them either, right?"

"No one has. I think the school is afraid after the innuendoes about them in the press. The press isn't above twisting things to fit their theories."

"So if you got this reporter an exclusive interview with the next best thing—someone who's recently visited the school, he'd owe you, right?"

Mahoney threw Dorsey's ball again and turned to face me. "What little scheme are you hatching now?"

"Kinda obvious, isn't it? You talk me into giving him an exclusive interview, and you get a bonus IOU. I'm feeling a little guilty about my visit to the school and directing your attention to Wong since it's gotten the school in trouble. I'd like to do something to help."

I received the following letter from Mrs. Higgins after the reporter's article ran in the paper.

"I cannot thank you enough for your support during this difficult time. Because of your positive attitude and enthusiasm about the work we do here, we have received

134

dozens of letters expressing regret for our situation and wishing us well.

Someone sent a copy of the article to a professional grant writer in California. He contacted us and said he would like to work with us to secure funds to finish building the new library. He was quite optimistic about being able to achieve that goal.

This positive input from the community has caused the Board of Directors and myself to reevaluate our policies toward public relations. In the interest of protecting our students from the prejudice the hearing or speech impaired often experience, we chose to seclude them. We think now that was a mistake. We should be building bridges for them, not creating a deeper abyss. Your visit taught us that. Both students and staff enjoyed interacting with you, and you clearly felt the same. I also think our aloofness helped cause the shadow of doubt that now hangs over us.

Come Christmas time, we plan to hold an open house for people to tour our school, meet our students, and see their accomplishments. I know you were particularly impressed with our music program. We have a bell choir, quite a good one, which will play carols during the open house as an example of their achievements.

I hope you are still planning to come back to meet with students interested in writing as we had discussed during your visit. Our doors are always open to you."

Wow! Did that letter make me feel good!

I grabbed the paper and ran to the office where Mahoney was supervising the unloading of boxes of wood flooring. We weren't ready to lay the flooring yet, but we'd run into a great sale and bought the materials early. Mahoney wanted to make sure the deliverymen stacked all the boxes in the middle of the room so they wouldn't be in the way for our second 'barn-raising.'

"Mahoney, have you seen this?"

He took the paper, but two deliverymen came through the door and he showed them where to stack the boxes.

"Do me a favor, Princess? We've only got a couple of more boxes to unload. Would you put on a fresh pot of coffee for me? I'll finish up here and be right with you." He handed the paper back to me.

I put on the coffee and sat down to read Mrs. Higgins's letter again. Two sentences jumped out at me. *"In the interest of protecting our students from the prejudice the hearing or speech impaired often experience, we chose to seclude them"* and *"I also think our aloofness helped cause the shadow of doubt that now hangs over us."*

Mahoney came in and poured himself a fresh cup of coffee. "Now what's so exciting in the paper?"

I showed him the article and helped myself to a banana while he read.

"That's my girl," he said when he finished.

"Focus on these sentences," I said and pointed out the two that had captured my attention.

"I think the first one, *'In the interest of protecting our students from the prejudice the hearing or speech impaired often experience, we chose to seclude them'* explains why she won't talk to anyone. To know that prejudice exists means she's probably experienced it herself."

"Makes sense. And she's afraid of running into it again."

"Now look at the other sentence. *'I also think our aloofness helped cause the shadow of doubt that now hangs over us.'* She realizes that her silence was more harmful than protective. I think she'll talk to you now."

"Maybe. I don't know. She doesn't exactly say she's

ready to cooperate with the investigation. Why do you think she'll talk to the police now?"

"Not the police—you. Because of this." I pointed to my wedding ring. "She's still reticent, but she trusts me. If you and I go together, just the two of us, you're police, but also my husband. I think she'll trust you too."

"It's certainly worth a try. Come here." He enfolded me in a bear hug. How secure I felt when he did that!

Chapter 30

Mrs. Higgins agreed to meet with Mahoney. She was hesitant to answer his questions at first, but after he assured her that he didn't believe she or the school were involved in any way, she opened up.

Mahoney began. Was she aware Mr. Wong was under investigation?

Yes, but why in the world would the police suspect Mr. Wong? He was such a timid little man. A bank robber? Shooting someone? No, she couldn't imagine that at all. Besides, he had visitors from out of town around that time. Didn't that give him an alibi of sorts?

Had she met his guests?

No. But he'd taken a week off from school to entertain them. How could he do that and commit a bank robbery at the same time?

Mahoney glanced over at me. A little naïve?

Wasn't it a bit unusual to take a week off from work to entertain guests?

Yes, but Mr. Wong had explained to her that they were coming all the way from China. It wasn't like they could visit any time they wanted. Closing the library for a week wasn't a great disruption to the school's routine, and Mr. Wong had spent so much of his personal time trying to find funding for the new library, that she saw no reason to deny the request.

Mahoney and I exchanged glances. Not four mute robbers—one mute and three who might not speak English.

Did she have the exact dates Wong had taken leave? She checked her records and gave Mahoney the dates.

The slightest of smiles flashed momentarily across Mahoney's face. See, Mahoney, you taught me well. I can pick up those tiny reactions. The bank robbery had occurred during Wong's absence from the school.

Had he acted any differently when he returned to work?

She didn't have a lot of contact with Mr. Wong on a daily basis. He mostly kept to himself in the library. But she had checked with him on the day of his return. He seemed quite happy and told her that he'd had a very successful week with his guests.

I had to butt in. Didn't she find the word 'successful' an odd choice?

Yes, but Mr. Wong's English wasn't perfect. He often used a word that communicated his intent, but was not the word a native speaker would use.

Was he good at his job?

Oh, yes, he was very dedicated to the library.

Did he get along well with the students and other staff?

As to the students, she'd never received any complaints about him. He wasn't the warmest person, too formal, but very competent at his job. As to the staff, as she'd said, he mostly kept to himself.

No special friends on the staff?

Not that she knew of.

Finally Mahoney asked if he could meet Mr. Wong.

Mrs. Higgins balked at that. She'd agreed to an interview with the police but did not feel it was proper to oblige any staff member to do so. What if the three of them walked to the library as though Mrs. Higgins were giving a tour? Well...

And Mahoney promised to keep communication to everyday topics—no 'police' questions. She didn't see any harm in that.

When we walked into the library, Mr. Wong stiffened. He signed to Mrs. Higgins. Not even a pretense of politeness this time.

"They are here on a tour of the school," Mrs. Higgins said aloud so as not to exclude us from the conversation.

Wong signed. "Yes, Mrs. Mahoney was here before, and this is her husband, Detective Mahoney."

Wong tossed the book he'd been holding and headed for the door.

"Mr. Wong," Mrs. Higgins called after him, "these people are our guests." He didn't stop.

Mrs. Higgins looked puzzled. "I am so sorry," she said. "I don't know why he acted like that. He's generally reserved, but not rude. It must be the pressure we are under. I will definitely speak to him about his behavior."

We heard a car start outside but couldn't see the parking lot. "Would you excuse me for a minute?" Mahoney said and left before Mrs. Higgins had a chance to answer.

I knew he was making a quick phone call to the department. He didn't need to see the car; the department already had all Wong's info on file. I needed to stall Mrs. Higgins while Mahoney phoned. I walked over to the window and looked out at the construction site. Not a worker in sight.

"I see work has stalled on the library," I said.

"Yes. When the bank manager called and said there may be some problem with the gift money and they couldn't disburse any more funds from our building fund account until the problem was cleared up, we had to stop the construction. Without the funding..." Her voice trailed off. "I don't understand any of this. Mr. Wong a bank robber? The school helping him?"

Mahoney returned. "I want to thank you so much for your cooperation Mrs. Higgins. We'll excuse ourselves now and let you get back to your work."

If she thought our departure a bit abrupt, she didn't say so. As we walked back to the front entrance, I said, "I'd like to send you a couple of possible dates to come meet with your students."

That cheered her up. "Please do." We shook hands at the door. "I'll look forward to hearing from you."

Mahoney practically raced to the car. I couldn't keep up with his long strides.

"Mahoney!"

He looked back. "Oh, sorry, Princess. I'm..."

"I know. But I'm afraid you'll drive off without me."

"I'd never..."

I caught up to him. We lived on the other side of town. The station was halfway between the school and our house. "Drive to the station."

"But I have to get you home."

"Have one of the uniforms drive me."

He squeezed my hand. "Thanks."

In the station parking lot, he'd take several long strides, stop and wait for me, then take long strides again. I finally waved my hand 'go, go' fashion. He rushed inside. I caught up to him at the entrance to the detectives' room where he was engrossed in a conversation with Bert.

"We had a patrol car in front of his house before he got there," Bert said.

"He saw it?"

"Oh, yah. He ran into his garbage pails pulling into the driveway. You really rattled him. What did you say to him?"

"Absolutely nothing. Never had a chance. He ran as soon as Mrs. Higgins said 'detective.' I think he felt safe in the school. But when Mrs. Higgins agreed to speak with us, he must have known she'd blow any chance of an alibi. Then I appeared."

"Arty and Mike went over there, but he refuses to answer the door. And we don't have cause to break in."

Lieutenant Palmer joined them. "We've got cruisers watching the place for now. Chances are he'll stay put until tonight and try to get out under cover of darkness. I want you two to go home and rest. It could be a long night. Be back here an hour before sunset. We'll finalize our plans then. If anything happens before then, we'll call." Palmer strode away.

I stood over to the side waiting. Bert finally saw me. "Oh, hi."

"Did my invisibility cloak fall off?"

Mahoney spun around. "Oh, honey, I'm sor…"

"Shhh. Let's go home."

Chapter 31

How do you tell a detective who's keyed up for a bust to rest? Impossible! I'd have to ask Molly if she knew any techniques.

About 4:00, Mahoney's phone rang. He headed for the door as he listened. "On my way," he said and disconnected. To me, he said, "Don't wait up for me," and disappeared.

I expected him to be gone most of the night, so I was surprised when he returned several hours later.

"It's over," he said collapsing to the couch. His body language said it wasn't a satisfactory ending.

"Tell me in order," I said, "from the time of the phone call."

The FBI had traced the money trail from the bank robbery to a business in San Francisco which was already under investigation for money laundering and had ties to China. The obvious question was why such a business would arrange to send money to a relatively unknown sign language school. The amount of the donation was only half what the robbers had taken, but half was still a very large cut. The other half, they assumed, was for services rendered. One of the officers in that company was named Peter Wong. The connections were strong enough to bring our Li Wong in for questioning.

"Peter Wong? A relative?"

"We suspect so. Of course, Wong is a common name, and there's the complication of his Anglicized first name. The FBI is searching records."

When the FBI and the Cedar Falls police tried to pick him up, Li Wong did not answer the door. They broke in and found Wong's body. He had hanged himself. He'd left a note on a table with only two words. "I failed." Finding the body was anti-climactic for the Cedar Falls P.D. who'd hoped to apprehend Blakely's shooter.

"How sad," I said.

Li Wong's passion for his library grew into such an obsession that it became not only the center of his life, but his sole motivation for living. When the police searched the premises, they found mounds of information on writing grants, rough drafts of the grants he'd applied for, and "sorry to inform you" letters on those he had submitted. Mahoney said they read much like the few examples we had seen of his writing.

Who knows how much that affected the rejection of his proposals? Might there have been a different outcome if he had asked someone to help him rewrite his broken English into accepted Standard English? His frustration led him to seek other misguided means of securing funding, and in the end, that didn't work either. I think he committed suicide, not out of fear of being caught or punished, but because he lost all hope.

"Yeah," Mahoney agreed. "We really wanted to question him and catch the others. We may never know who actually shot Blakely." His mind was still on the case.

The FBI took full charge of the investigation after Li Wong's death, since Cedar Falls had no jurisdiction in California. They searched Wong's home for evidence of the robbery and his connection to Peter Wong or the other three robbers. They also fingerprinted the house in case any of Li Wong's visitors had left prints behind. The circumstances frustrated the Cedar Falls P.D. because they could not close the case, but cases go that way sometimes.

Following procedure, the FBI took the amount of the donated 'gift' to the school out of the school's building fund account, returned it to the bank, and unfroze the school's account. Mrs. Higgins is working with the grant writer to find new funding. I haven't forgotten my promise to return to the Sign Language Center to meet with students interested in writing.

Our second office 'barn-raising' went without a hitch. I invited Jennie's dog Hercules over for a play-date so Dorsey would have some company and not feel the need to help the men and get underfoot.

Mahoney and I picked out our office furniture and it arrived a couple of days after the barn-raising: two desks—although mine is much larger—with chairs, a small bookcase near mine for reference materials that need to be close at hand, and two reading chairs with side tables. A closet holds supplies and my research materials so they don't clutter up the room.

Because of Mahoney's arm, we hired a mason to lay the flagstone patio. It curves gracefully around the back yard from behind the office past the kitchen area and a rear door that we only used to put out the garbage. Now that door opens onto a large patio perfect for entertaining. I'll write a letter to Santa asking him to leave our new patio furniture and a grill for Mahoney on the patio instead of bringing it down the chimney where it might get stuck.

Behind the office is a seating area where I can take a break for think time or simply to stretch out the kinks from sitting at the computer for too long.

Dorsey likes the new patio; it's become a favorite resting spot. I didn't like him lying on the cold flagstone, so Mahoney and I bought him a bed. We selected the location for the bed, but when we put it down, Dorsey promptly dragged it closer to the office doors where he could see me when I worked. Woof, woof, he said as he curled up into it. "This is great!"

I now dedicate my mornings to writing. Some days when my muse is talking fast, I stay at the computer all day. No more having to take notes for my next session, to put away my work materials, and to tidy up my desk at the end of the day. Now I can just close the door on my mess. Of course, I still need to set the alarm on those marathon days to warn me when it's 'Mahoney time.'

The girls still meet regularly for lunch, and the guys tease us about what project we'll dream up next.

Life has finally settled down to a normal—and safe—routine compared to the last year. My home had been bombed and burned to the ground. I'd been shot at; Mahoney had been shot. The two people arrested for the shooting had also stalked me. Mahoney has regained the strength in his arm, but would always have that scar to remind us. More than our fair share of mayhem, right? Such horrible things couldn't happen again. Could they?

#####

About The Author

I was born in New York, but the lure of open spaces brought me west, and I now call Arizona home. Throughout my professional life as an educator and newspaper editor, my passion has always been writing. My other passion is exploring all the West has to offer, and I am often RVing down the road with my cat Charlie.

Books by the Author

Mahoney and Me Series

Stopping in Lonely Places An author departs in her RV on a leisurely book signing tour. A stop for lunch at an isolated spot along the road changes her life when a robber pulls up behind her van and threatens her. A stray border collie intervenes and scares off the aggressor. Of course, she can't leave the dog behind after he saved her, and the collie eagerly accepts her invitation to jump in the van. That chance encounter with the robber leads to his pursuit of her for reasons she doesn't understand. When she meets Mahoney, the detective assigned to her case, sparks fly between them.

Mahoney and Me Cedar Falls is turned upside down by a bank robbery, kidnapping, and shooting of a police officer. While Mahoney investigates those crimes, the narrator has to contend with a wicked love triangle involving Bethany, a woman so fixated on Mahoney that she believed they were a couple, and the boyfriend fixated on her who goes after Mahoney, hoping to get him out of Bethany's life. Will the blatant second cop shooting outside the police station end their wedding plans?

Caught in Lies Identity theft, impersonation, and murder lead Detective Mahoney and the narrator across the country to New York to find the connection between two 'look-alikes.' Are they responsible for killing Homer Hunter? Or will a crank call from a mentally disturbed youth lead them to the murderer? Did he convert into action his belief that old people are useless and should die? Meanwhile, Mahoney's former girlfriend shows up in town and wants to reunite with him.

Other Books

A Date To Die For The stalker spots Stacey on her first day at Hollis High. Instant attraction. He begins by following her, secretly taking pictures, phoning her and hanging up. As she makes friends with other students, he feels threatened and responds with bolder actions—slashing car tires, breaking into her house. Time is running out for her as the stalker plans his last desperate attempt to "own" her. Be prepared for an ending you won't expect!

Calico Kate is historical fiction set in the late 1800s, in Calico, California, considered the richest silver mining town in the West. From the time Kate steps off the train from New York City, she steps into California history. Her adventures mimic life in a mining town from witnessing a shooting in a saloon, to fighting a fire that threatens to destroy the town, to solving a murder mystery.

When the Squeaking Starts... When Mr. Carlson buys an old Victorian mansion, he has no idea he's also inheriting its ghosts. His daughter Sandy, however, quickly discovers something's amiss. Sandy must find the truth behind these warring ghosts, as she is caught in the middle of their battles. The story unfolds in two time periods: chapters alternate between the new owners and the former owners whose struggles continue past their deaths.

History buffs might be interested in an eight-volume series of nonfiction booklets about *The Early History of Sunland, California*, now in their second printing. The town started during the Land Boom of the 1880s, when the completion of the transcontinental railroad started a movement westward. While Sunland's struggle mirrored the basic needs of many beginning Western towns, it also had its unique stories—a farmer who doubled as a hit man for the Mafia, a resident who committed "...the boldest train robbery that ever took place in Southern California..." Only available in print.

Author contact: www.maryleetiernan.com

Made in the USA
San Bernardino, CA
12 April 2014